AUG 21 2021

NO LONGER PROPERTY OF
SEATTLE PUBLIC LIBRARY

D0955396

NIKKI TESLA AND THE TRAITORS OF THE LOST SPARK

ALSO BY JESS KEATING

Nikki Tesla and the Ferret-Proof Death Ray

Nikki Tesla and the Fellowship of the Bling

NIKKI TESLA AND THE TRAITORS OF THE LOST SPARK

JESS KEATING
ILLUSTRATED BY LISSY MARLIN

SCHOLASTIC PRESS

NEW YORK

Text copyright © 2020 by Jess Keating
Illustrations by Lissy Marlin, copyright © 2020 Scholastic Inc.

All rights reserved. Published by Scholastic Press, an imprint of Scholastic Inc.,
Publishers since 1920. SCHOLASTIC, SCHOLASTIC PRESS, and associated logos
are trademarks and/or registered trademarks of Scholastic Inc.

The publisher does not have any control over and does not assume
any responsibility for author or third-party websites or their content.

No part of this publication may be reproduced, stored in a retrieval
system, or transmitted in any form or by any means, electronic, mechanical,
photocopying, recording, or otherwise, without written permission of the publisher.
For information regarding permission, write to Scholastic Inc., Attention:
Permissions Department, 557 Broadway, New York, NY 10012.

This book is a work of fiction. Names, characters, places, and incidents are either
the product of the author's imagination or are used fictitiously, and any
resemblance to actual persons, living or dead, business establishments,
events, or locales is entirely coincidental.

Library of Congress Cataloging-in-Publication Data available

ISBN 978-1-338-61476-3

10 9 8 7 6 5 4 3 2 1   20 21 22 23 24

Printed in the U.S.A.   23
First edition, July 2020
Book design by Keirsten Geise

To all my amazing readers:
Not only are you brave and brilliant,
but you've got wonderful taste in books.

(But seriously, it's a joy to write for you all.
Thanks for coming along for the ride!)

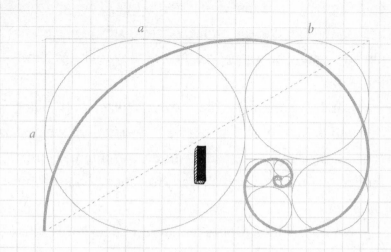

Ahh, vacation.

I stretched my arms above my head, letting the movement and airflow cool some of the clammy sweat from my body.

Know what my favorite part of vacation was? Besides the little capuchin monkeys chattering in the trees above me?

There were no disasters.

No evil villains trying to take over the world.

No ridiculously impossible odds to face, and no world-saving missions to complete.

It was only me, my family, and the huge orchid balanced above my ear. Relaxing in the teeming jungle with chirping birds and insects all around us. Though to be honest, the fact that the orchid wouldn't stay in place was already getting on my nerves. I was ready to throw it into the ocean.

"Can't I hold *onto* the flowers instead of being decorated in them? I'm not a flowerpot," I whined. Pickles, my ferret, seemed to agree, swiping the wispy tendril of flower as she shifted from her perch on my shoulder.

"No way, kiddo." Mom's mouth turned up into a satisfied smirk.

If you'd ever seen my mom before today, you probably wouldn't have recognized her. She usually had what I like to call Momface—a combination of weary and paranoid, probably because she spent most of her time worried about whether or not one of my latest inventions was going to blow up the house.

Understandable, considering it was known to happen on occasion.

But ever since my dad had come out of hiding from the police (and us!) after being framed for attempted murder seven years ago? Mom was a breezy, smiling, walking ray of sunshine.

"We only get to do this once, so everything's going to be special. And if you insist on Pickles riding on your shoulder during the ceremony, she's going to have to get used to the flowers . . ." She handed me a cluster of messy wildflowers as a placeholder bouquet. "Both in your hands *and* your hair!"

I rolled my eyes. "Technically you're not doing this *once*," I reminded her. "This is your second time walking down the aisle. To the same guy, even. What's the point of getting married *again*? You never got divorced or anything. He just disappeared."

"The point, my dear child," she said, "is a new start. We've gone seven years without your dad, and we want to make his return special. Plus, this time, you'll be there with us. It's the start of a new chapter in the book of our lives!" She lifted her hands dramatically.

"The book of our lives needs another lemonade, not a wedding!" I licked my parched lips, trying to remember where I'd left my water bottle.

I should probably explain the past few months, in case you haven't been keeping track in my official government records. Actually, you know what? Explaining would take too long. Let me sum it up:

I'm a genius. I got shipped off to a boarding school that turned out to be a secret government-run place called Genius Academy helmed by a tough, no-nonsense lady called Martha. The students' job, to put it bluntly, is to save the world. We use quick thinking, prodigious expertise, and a good dose of luck to protect Earth and its inhabitants from threats. I'll admit it: It's totally fun.

But don't let the fact that we're geniuses make you think we're all the same.

Nope, Genius Academy is an equal-opportunity agency, representing different kinds of brilliant minds. Some of us excel at inventing and building dangerous weapons (that's me!), while others are experts at stuff like music, physics, chemistry, leadership, or reading people. Or, if you're like my friend-and-possibly-boyfriend, Leo da Vinci, you're good at everything. (Which is completely unfair, if you ask me.)

Anyway. So, before I joined the Academy—seven years ago, as I already mentioned—my dad was all over the news for blowing up his lab. The police found plans for a bomb that he was developing to use to hurt a bunch of people. But guess what? He was framed! By an evil dude who wanted to sell one of Dad's cool inventions for boatloads of cash.

I know! How rude, right?

To make this long story short, he disappeared to keep me and my mom safe, but my friends from Genius Academy helped me clear his name, so he's back in the picture now.

That's great because it means I finally have my family together again, and we can let go of some pretty awful stuff from the past.

But it's not so great because it means I've had to endure my parents basically making out all the time, "reconnecting" after so many years apart. Barf!

Don't ask me why they couldn't reconnect by going out to a fancy, candlelit dinner like regular long-lost soul mates. Nope, they wanted to get away from it all. And I guess "it all" means air-conditioning and flat-screen televisions. As you can probably tell from the vines and monkeys surrounding me, I'm not at the Academy anymore.

Welcome to the Monteverde Cloud Forest! Home to over four hundred species of birds, one hundred species of mammals, and one nerdy genius with a sunburn. Oh, and my parents, who are now rehearsing for their upcoming (second) wedding, where they're going to renew their vows and profess their love in holy matrimony.

My job today was to practice walking down the aisle alongside my mom at the right tempo. You'd think that being a genius would mean I'd be good at this, but the truth is, I could hardly balance on the tiny heels Mom had bought me to go with my bridesmaid dress. I've seen some people wear heels that are three inches tall without breaking their necks—how do they do it?!

I mean that literally: I've done the calculations, and the physics of walking on heels doesn't add up.

"So when you hear the second bar of the music, that's when we go." Mom gripped my elbow tightly, but her face was all smiling sunshine. Seeing Mom so happy after so many years of sadness was pretty great . . . even if it was hard on my feet.

Just then, Pickles chattered sharply in my ear and scurried down my arm, using her sharp claws to push off me as she catapulted to the ground. A flash of chocolate-brown and white, she bolted off in the direction of our hotel.

"Ouch!" I yelped, stumbling on my heels.

Mom held me steady and stared after Pickles. "What's up with her?"

I chewed my lip. "I'm not sure." I squinted against

the dappled sun streaming through the jungle leaves as a last flick of her tail disappeared around the curving trail. A low buzz of anxiety started to quiver inside my stomach.

"Mind if I go see what's up?" I asked Mom, trying to keep the edge of nervousness from my voice. "She's not usually like this. Not unless . . ."

The chatter of the jungle got louder in my ears. Pickles didn't race off like that unless she was motivated by something—or *someone*.

Mom took the bouquet from my hands. "Maybe the hotel staff has been sneaking her treats! Go ahead, sweetie. We've got a week until the wedding. Tons of time to practice."

"Thanks," I said. "Be right back!"

Kicking off my uncomfortable shoes, I darted after Pickles, my bare feet skidding on the path as I arrived at the cute little hotel my family was staying at for the next week.

"Pickles!" I yelled through the vivid green trees. "Where'd you go?" I clicked my tongue and clapped my hands, trying to get her attention. Usually, if I made noises like this, she'd think I had food and race back to me.

But this time . . . *nothing*.

Continuing through the hotel doors, I hoped someone at the front desk had seen her. Would they kick us out of here if she caused trouble? I plastered on a fake smile in hopes of endearing myself to the staff.

"Excuse me," I said, ducking under the ornamental tree by the door to reach the receptionist. "I'm looking for— *Oh!*"

The receptionist wasn't there. Instead, Pickles sat perched atop the shoulder of someone else.

Someone who should have been thousands of miles away . . .

"Hi, Nikki!" Charlie Darwin lifted her arms and danced in place. Then five other faces popped up from behind the counter, like they were celebrating a surprise birthday party.

Only it *definitely* wasn't my birthday.

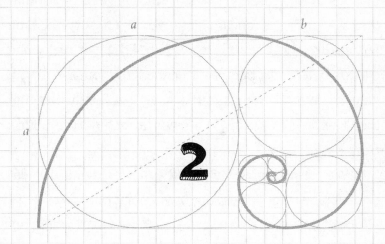

"What are you guys doing here?!" I reached over to give Charlie a hug, then made my way down the rest of the line to greet Mary Shelley, Grace O'Malley, Adam "Mo" Mozart, Bert Einstein, and, of course, Leo. My six genius buddies were a long way from Genius Academy. That could only mean one thing.

Trouble.

"Thought you could get rid of us that easy, huh?" Leo's eyes twinkled, sending my stomach into a flutter. He had this ridiculous way of setting off butterflies inside me. Ever since he'd kissed me on the rooftop of our last mission, I had to work extra hard not to giggle or blush when he looked at me. "It's going to take more than a vacation in the Cloud Forest to hide from us!" he said cheerfully.

"It's great to see you all," I said. A rush of adrenaline warmed my chest. I'd never been surprised by friends like this before. Then again, I'd never really *had* friends before. I'd been at the Academy for less than a year, but already my classmates felt like family. But that didn't explain why they'd shown up behind the hotel's front desk.

"We know you're supposed to be enjoying a vacation," Grace said. "We *all* are, I will point out."

Bert huffed with annoyance. "*I* was perfecting my spectral cloak," he said. "It's going to be the most advanced camouflage technology ever. And then, *boom*—there's Grace at my door!" He narrowed his eyes at her, pouting.

Grace ignored him. "I had no choice," she said. "Martha sent me. Something's come up, and she asked me to round up the team to help. Sorry, Nikki, but you need to come with us." Grace blinked at me, no trace of amusement on her face. "Like, now."

"What?!" I glanced behind me, hoping my mother hadn't followed me in. My parents understood what went on at Genius Academy, but there was no way that they'd be okay with me taking off in the middle of their wedding rehearsal.

"I can't randomly disappear," I said. I ducked my chin down, keeping my voice low. "We've got a fancy dinner tonight, and the wedding is in less than a week. I'm supposed to be practicing my walk right now."

"Is walking really that hard for you?" Mo questioned, tilting his head.

Mary shot him a look. "You try it in heels."

"Sorry, Tesla." Grace gave me a half-hearted shrug, but I didn't miss the glint of amusement as her gaze flicked above my ear. I'd forgotten about the orchid stuck there. I pawed it out of my hair and twisted it in my fingers awkwardly.

"We've been given strict orders. Martha *promised* to make it up to your parents and explain everything." Grace checked her watch. "But right now? We've got exactly three minutes to get you in the car out back. Or else."

I lifted my hands to my hips. I'd already decided. There was no way I was leaving my parents. "Or else *what*?"

Grace cracked her knuckles while Mo fiddled with the tiny bell on the countertop. A muted, tinny chime sounded in the air. "Or else we kidnap you," she said.

I cackled. "Sure, that sounds reasonable."

Bert grinned eagerly while Leo stared at his feet. Nobody was laughing with me.

"Wait, for real?" I choked. "Martha told you to *kidnap* me if I didn't cooperate?"

Grace shrugged again.

"I'm afraid so," Mo said. Rounding the corner of the front desk, he scooped me up and tossed me over his shoulder like a sack of potatoes. The others giggled and stepped out of his way as he moved easily toward the door, despite my arguments.

"HEY!" I yelped. "Put me down! You can't go around picking up people! I'll come with you, okay?!"

Mo grinned, setting me down with a thud. "Sorry," he said, pointing to the others. "They made me do it."

I wrung my hands in frustration and smoothed out my clothes, dusting off the indignation. "Can I at least tell my parents? Or grab my suitcase? Or *shoes*? Where exactly are we going?"

Grace barely acknowledged me as she breezed past the group and out the door, holding it open for us to follow. "We've already packed your stuff. You can thank Charlie for that."

Charlie lifted her hand in a mock salute. "Hotel door locks are delightfully easy to pick," she said. "I knew you'd want your notebook and stuff." She reached down by her feet and tossed me a backpack.

I debated making a run for it so I could at least tell my parents we'd gotten a new mission. Genius Academy hadn't exactly been the safest place in the world lately, and I was certain Mom would instantly assume the worst if I disappeared.

Grace must have noticed my hesitation. "Seriously, Nikki. I promise that Martha will explain everything to them. They'll understand once they find out why we had to leave."

"I hope that will make three of us, then," I muttered.

I held Pickles tightly in my arms as I got into the brown van that waited for us. As soon as we had all piled inside and the door slid shut, the driver hit the gas, sending a trail of dust flailing behind us.

My stomach lurched as I dug through the backpack and pulled out the sneakers that Charlie had packed for me, slipping them onto my feet. Letting the breeze from the open window wash over my face, two unshakable facts rose to the surface of my mind.

One: I should have known that disappearing into the Costa Rican jungle wouldn't be enough to keep Martha away. When you're responsible for saving the world, you don't ever really get a day off.

And two: My parents were going to absolutely lose their minds. With only a week until their wedding, I'd be lucky if they ever forgave me.

But I forced myself to ignore the bumpy dirt road disappearing behind me. If my friends had their heads in the game, I would, too.

"Okay," I said finally. "Let's hear it."

A familiar voice came from the driver's seat, sending the zip of a chill through me. "I'm afraid your vacation is over, Ms. Tesla."

I blinked in surprise. "Martha?! Since when do you make house calls? Shouldn't you be at the Academy, organizing our next move?"

Glancing at Leo, a new layer of sweat began to prickle on my skin. If the others knew what was wrong, they weren't letting on. With Martha here in person, whatever was going on had to be *big*.

"What's the mission?" I demanded.

Martha's eyes appeared in the rearview mirror, staring me down.

"I'm sorry for gathering all of you on such short notice," she said. "You know I wouldn't do this unless it was entirely necessary."

"Martha, you said once we got everyone assembled, you'd tell us what's going on." The muscles in Grace's neck were tight as she spoke. "Whatever it is, we can handle it."

Martha pressed her foot heavy on the gas, sending us jerking back in our seats as the van tore through the jungle.

"*It*," Martha said softly, "is the worst we've ever seen."

"The worst *what* you've ever seen?" Leo pressed.

Martha's brown eyes appeared in the rearview mirror once more, the bright Costa Rican sunlight revealing dark circles beneath them.

"Biological warfare," she said. "The end of humanity as we know it."

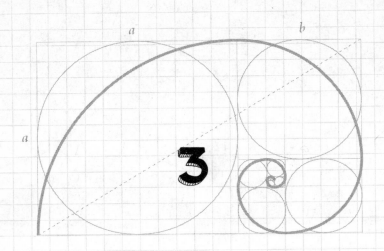

3

Usually, when Martha gives us a new assignment, she starts with a little backstory about the global disaster at hand. She uses the fancy computer in her office, with lots of flashy pictures and evidence, to tell us something's been stolen, someone's up to no good, the world's in unimaginable danger. That sort of thing.

But this time, she pulled over at a small thatched-roof house about seventy miles away to give us the lowdown. It was just the eight of us in a musty, sweaty jungle cabin on a washed-out trail in the Costa Rican rain forest.

Once we were all safely tucked away, she passed out bottles of water and carefully weighed what she wanted to tell us.

"I wouldn't pull you away from your families unless it was entirely necessary," Martha finally said, her face grim. "But there have been casualties."

Mary gasped. "Casualties?" Her mouth tipped into a frown. "Who died?"

"Several of our undercover agents. You see, for the past four years, we've been investigating suspects who specialize in biological experimentation. In particular, tracking someone who goes by V. We believe his name to be Victor. The few bits of rogue intelligence we dug up on him tell us he's operating on his own and experimenting with some highly dangerous materials. Last year for the first time we were able to hack into his computer. But that's when things went . . . awry."

"Awry . . . meaning people died?" Leo clarified.

Martha paused again. "Yes. Victor learned we were investigating him. He somehow accessed our agents' false identities and their real names and addresses. We believe he used that information to target the agents who were investigating him."

The silence in the room grew heavy, and the low drone of buzzing flies seemed to intensify. For all the craziness our adventures entailed, it was easy to forget we worked for a secret agency whose job it was to fight *very* dangerous people. We'd been lucky so far, but sometimes, people got hurt.

Or worse.

Martha pulled a small folder from her bag and set it on the table. "This is what Victor was trying to protect: plans for one of the most dangerous viruses known to man. When infected, humans become imbued with extraordinary strength and reflexes."

Bert perked up. "Like mutants?" He shifted in excitement. "Super humans?"

"Don't get too excited, Mr. Einstein," Martha said. "The incredible abilities are a by-product of the virus, not the intention." She tapped her phone for a moment and tipped the screen toward us. "The effects we're talking about are violent and unpredictable." She pressed play on the video.

A grainy image of a man in what looked to be a sterile laboratory environment paced angrily across the screen. He shook his fists aggressively, as though he couldn't contain his movements, while his head and neck twitched awkwardly. It was almost like he was fighting for control of his own body.

"Oh no," Mary whispered, recoiling at the moving images.

The man on the screen raised his fists toward the ceiling, then turned into a flash—a literal *flash*—across the room, bolting from one side to the next.

It was a video I wouldn't have believed—or *couldn't* have believed—if I didn't know Martha and how seriously she took her job. If I hadn't already seen impossible things with my own eyes.

It was a video of a man becoming a monster.

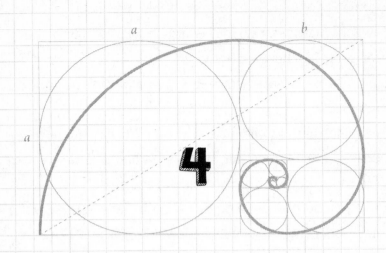

"Whoa!" Charlie said, leaning closer. "Is this *real*?!" The man had started punching the wall, crumbling the concrete to bits under his fists. Shards of broken glass from the laboratory window didn't faze him as he tore through the room like a hurricane, wrenching through the glass with his bare, bleeding hands.

"*Ackkk!* This is awful!" Mary cringed, covering her eyes at the mess and gore.

As disturbing as it was, I couldn't look away from the screen. "It reminds me of Dad's ring," I muttered.

The rest of the group nodded in agreement. A few months earlier, we'd tracked down a ring that my own father had invented that allowed its user to turn into *any* kind of creature using cellular realignment.

It sounds cool, right? The ability to become anything you want? But the reality is terrifying. There are some things that human beings should never be able to do.

Grace frowned. "So Victor created a virus that turns people into superhuman mutants..."

"It changes human biology to create spontaneous physiological accelerated reactionary kinesthetics."

"*S.P.A.R.K.,*" Mary whispered. The color drained quickly from her sweaty cheeks.

"Yes," Martha agreed. "As Mary's so cleverly noted, we're calling it the Spark virus. Victor has generated it in the form of a serum that can be either injected into one's bloodstream or spread via airborne pathogens."

Charlie let out a low whistle. "That sounds... dangerous."

Bert leaned forward, stopping the footage on the screen and staring closer. "So when you found out about it, Victor got upset, tracked down a bunch of Academy agents, and... killed them," he clarified. "And now you can't send more of your usual agents after him because he knows all their identities."

"I'm afraid so." Martha swallowed a gulp from her water bottle and wiped her damp forehead. "Only your parents and a handful of high-ranking government officials know about Genius Academy, and that information is guarded by the president herself. There is no way that Victor knows anything about you. Which is why you're the only ones he won't see coming."

I was beginning to see her plan.

"So what do you need us to do?" Grace asked.

"We've learned that he's planning to visit the Tower of London."

Charlie perked up. "Do we get to go?" A small glimmer of excitement grew behind her eyes.

"Yes. You'll go to England and find him," Martha said. "Victor's movements have been erratic, and without our top agents able to work on the investigation, he's been far too easy to lose. He pops up in one country, then reappears days later in another. In order to figure out what he's planning to do with his virus, I need you to tag him."

Mo made a face. "Tag him with what? A tracker? Won't that be easy for him to find?"

"Our research team has been working on an aerosol tracking system," she said, her cheeks lifting in a smile. "Using colorless, odorless nanoparticle technology. Basically, if you spray him, he'll glow when viewed through our global surveillance tracking system."

"Spray paint?" I repeated. "You want us to tag him with magic paint?"

Martha sniffed. "I assure you, it's not magic. Just science."

She was right. The two weren't that far apart when you got right down to it.

"Right," I said. "So we go to London, find this Victor guy at the Tower, and then spray-paint him. That doesn't seem so bad."

Grace sat taller. She was ready to get moving. "Do we know what he looks like?"

"We have surveillance footage that might be helpful, but it isn't terribly clear."

I stroked Pickles's fur anxiously as the others exchanged glances.

"What's he going to be doing at the Tower of London?" Leo asked. "Does it have anything to do with the Spark virus?"

"I wish I knew," Martha admitted. Her forehead creased with worry. "It could be a meeting with an associate or a potential customer for the virus, or even just a diversion—one more stop on a wild-goose chase to distract us from his real agenda."

"Oh, that's great!" Bert said. He took off his glasses and used the hem of his shirt to wipe them clean before shoving them back onto his face. "We're expected to fol-low this mystery man without knowing a thing about what he even *looks* like. And if we do somehow figure it out, we're supposed to spray-paint him so you guys can see what he does with this mutant-making virus of his?" He clasped his hands tightly together, turning his knuck-les white.

Grace bit her lip to keep from laughing. "That's kind of the job, dude."

Bert let out a heavy sigh. "Just checking."

Martha's tone softened. "I recognize that this situa-tion isn't ideal. But there's one more thing you should know before agreeing to this mission. As much as I'd like to protect you all, you *must* have all the information before you get involved."

"What's left? An anonymous mad scientist. A virus that makes people mutants. And a trip to London. What more do we need?" Charlie draped her arm over the back of Mary's chair beside her.

"The Spark virus," Martha said. She looked down at her phone for a moment, swiping through the images. Finally, she held it up to show us a video of what ap-peared to be round cells flickering and twitching under a microscope. "I told you that extraordinary strength was simply a side effect of the virus, not the goal. Watch what happens when a human comes into contact with it."

Martha set the phone down, and we all leaned forward for a better view. Compared to the guy punching walls, this video wasn't graphic. It was basically a bunch of normal human cells with some spiky-looking smaller cells circulating around them. But suddenly the spiky cells started jabbing the regular, healthy-looking cells.

"Oh, *ew*," Grace said. "What are they doing?"

"That's the virus," Martha said. She paused the video. The healthy cells had changed from round and solid to withered and dark. She tapped the phone screen with a fingernail, pointing to one of the spiky virus cells. "This is the virus. This is what we're facing if we don't succeed."

Bert's face turned a shade of greenish gray. "So the real intention of the virus is to . . . kill people? That's the goal?"

"Yes." Martha let the full truth settle over us. "The *spark* temporarily gives people superior strength. But once that strength fades—usually within a matter of a day—it begins to destroy the cells it previously enhanced. The Spark virus kills its hosts one hundred percent of the time if a proper antidote isn't introduced."

She glanced at her watch again before continuing. "If you don't want to accept this mission, I will understand. Nobody is being forced here."

An eerie silence surrounded us as we all exchanged glances. Even Pickles stayed quiet, like she knew the severity of what Martha was saying.

I won't lie, a big part of me wanted to hop off my chair and make a run for it. My parents' faces swam in front of me, eager to welcome me back to their wedding planning, going on with their lives like usual. I could have walked out of there and everything could have gone back to normal.

But then I realized: Without us, any hope of normal would be gone for everyone on the planet. If other agents couldn't protect people, then we had to do it. Could I live with myself if this horrible virus was unleashed into the world? I didn't think I could.

What choice was there?

"I don't see any of us leaving, so . . ." Bert mused. He rubbed his hands together. "What's a little biological warfare between friends, anyway?"

A small smile grew on Martha's face.

"So it's settled, then?" Charlie looked around expectantly, her ponytail swishing. "We're going to London?!"

"There's one more thing," Grace said. Her gaze was fixed on Martha. "We're going to need you to tell us why you keep looking at that watch of yours."

Mary tilted her head, as though reading every line on Martha's face, like she would the page of a book. "You're not supposed to be telling us any of this, are you, Martha?"

Martha opened her mouth to answer, but a sharp crack outside the cabin sent us skittering from the table, arranging ourselves instinctively with our backs to the far wall.

Someone was coming for us.

"Martha!" Grace's voice was a sharp whisper as her arms shot out to shield the rest of us. Leo and Mo shifted forward, their fingers flexed and ready for whatever faced us beyond the door.

"Who is it?!" Grace asked. "Who's after us?"

Martha rolled her shoulders once before answering,

shifting her neck to stretch it. "They're not after you," she said. "There was some . . . disagreement about whether to involve Genius Academy in this matter. Given that we've lost full-fledged agents, my colleagues didn't believe you'd be up to the task. But we don't have a choice here. They suspected I'd reach out to you for help. And now they're coming to stop me."

I jumped as a rustling sound in the bushes was followed by the nearby squawk of some sort of rain forest bird. Whatever was out there had scared the local wildlife.

"Tell us what to do," I said to Martha. I positioned Pickles on my shoulder so she'd be ready for a quick getaway. "How do we get you away from here safely?"

"The back sounds clear so far," Mo suggested.

Reflected light flashed on the surface of Bert's glasses as he darted a look behind us. "We could—"

"No!" Martha interrupted. "You're not to worry about my safety. I'm going to create a diversion, and when I do, your job is to get out of here in one piece. Finish the mission. No matter what anyone else says. I'll meet you in London. Use our safe house there if you encounter any trouble."

My legs grew weak, and my mind raced to argue with her. Surely she couldn't be serious—we couldn't leave her behind.

"There must be some other way," Leo said. "Martha, let us help!"

With a quick shake of her head, Martha threw her phone toward the front of the cabin, along with the folder of research.

"Leave through the back," she instructed as she tossed a small cartridge onto the small pile. Instantly, the cartridge began to sizzle and smoke, sending up a ferocious shriek. Flames ignited the papers and licked the air. Thick smoke filled the cabin in a blink, and Martha stepped into it, disappearing as a wide beam of light sliced through the haze. The door of the cabin had opened, but whoever had come for Martha remained obscured. The only thing I could make out was the silhouette of a gun in one of their hands.

Leo's fingers threaded through mine and yanked my arm sharply.

"Come on!" he said, tugging me toward where the others were escaping out a window on the southern wall. But no matter what I did, I couldn't force my feet to move.

"We can't leave her!" I shouted, desperate to chase after her.

But Leo and the others were quicker to accept what I couldn't.

What choice did we have? Ignore Martha's orders and get caught? We'd never be able to finish our mission, which wasn't an option.

With one final look at the blaze behind me, I turned on my heels and followed Leo, leaping out the shattered window and landing on the spongy ground.

The others had taken off as fast as their legs would carry them, but Grace remained behind, holding a large leafy branch in her hands.

"Go!" Her eyes flashed wildly. "I'll cover our tracks!"

I did the only thing left to do.

I ran.

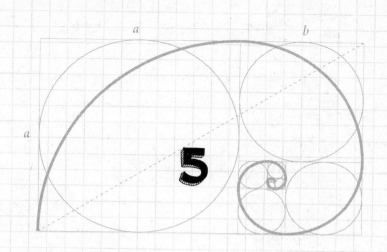

5

We spent the next two days anxiously watching our backs, meticulously planning, and trying to ignore Bert's constant stream of trivia about England.

Seriously, did you know that there are over one thousand castles in England? And that all the swans in the River Thames technically belong to the queen? And that King Edward the Third once attended a fancy party dressed up as a pheasant?

Thanks to Bert, now you do.

Considering my only experience of London comes from Paddington Bear movies, I wasn't quite sure what to expect. Bears with marmalade, for sure, and maybe some of those wacky-looking guards in the red coats and funny hats?

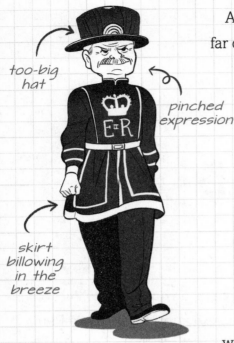

too-big
hat

pinched
expression

skirt
billowing
in the
breeze

As it turned out, I wasn't far off.

I mean, there were no talking bears. That was definitely a let-down. But the Tower of London *was* surrounded by guards, not to mention what seemed like a million tourists eager to get a peek inside medieval life.

Oh, and in case you're wondering, calling it the "Tower" is kind of a misnomer, because even though there are towers there, the whole thing is actually a castle.

We'd devised our next move on the plane. Because we didn't know what Victor looked like, we had to go with the clues Martha had given us and the pack she'd left for us on the Academy plane.

Each of us had a canister of the tracking spray and strict instructions to focus on the area of the castle where the Crown Jewels were displayed. Martha believed that whatever his reason for being there, Victor would stick to where the tourists were most congested to protect his anonymity. It's easy to blend in when there's lots of people around.

Our only job was to sniff out suspicious characters and tag them with our spray. From there, we'd have to hope that Martha was able to talk her way out of trouble and convince the government to use their global tracking system to find him.

Easy peasy, right?

"Okay, everyone. Gather round." Grace glanced up at the cloudless blue sky before giving us our instructions.

We stood on the flat, tidy stone path outside the entrance to the Crown Jewels tower. The breeze was cool, but there was a sense of warmth and excitement in the air from the bustling, happy crowds of tourists surrounding us. Stale castle air mingled with the sharp scents of coffee and damp stone, adding to the tense swell of nerves in my stomach.

"Once we're inside, everyone is a suspect, okay?" Grace continued. "I want to break up into teams. Mary and Nikki, you take the southern part of the display. Leo, Charlie, you take north. Bert and I will take west, and Mo, you're east. We're looking for anyone who matches the description from the surveillance footage: male, dark brown hair, about six foot two. He might be wearing glasses like in Martha's sketch, but maybe not."

Bert shielded his face from the sun. "Yeah, that narrows it down, doesn't it?"

I bit my lip at the sight of several men matching the description wandering by with their families.

"Remember, you're looking for more than physical appearance," Grace said. "Our suspect will probably be observant and suspicious. All we can do is hope that he stands out to one of us. Stay in communication at all times, okay?"

On the way up the crowded hallway to the Crown Jewels, Bert read off more random facts from his pamphlet.

"Did you know that the Tower of London is only a nickname?" he asked, pointing to the page in his hand. "It's technically called Her Majesty's Royal Palace and Fortress, the Tower of London." He sniffed, rolling off the words in a false posh accent similar to Charlie's.

"For a fortress, you'd think they'd invest in wider hallways," Mo huffed, angling himself away from a family of six squeezing in to pass by us.

I giggled with Mary, who climbed the stairs behind me. Since arriving in London, we'd all done our best to keep a brave face for whatever was to come, but something about the tightness behind her smile made me worry.

As her best friend, I knew my job wasn't only to stop evil villains, it was also to make sure she was all right.

I decided to take advantage of the chance to talk to her without the others listening. "Hey," I said under my breath. "Are you okay?"

She pulled the sunglasses from her face and slid them up past her forehead, tidying back her thick hair. "Yep! I'm good!" she said brightly.

That was my first clue that something was still wrong. Charlie was the perky one, not Mary.

"Are you sure?" I went on. "Ever since Costa Rica, you've been a little quiet."

She took a few more steps and wrinkled her nose. "I'm always quiet, you know that."

"Sure," I said. "I guess you seem *more* quiet than usual. You can tell me if you're scared, you know?"

"I'm *fine*, Nikki," she said. "I swear."

I kept my mouth shut, hoping she'd continue. It was one of the tips that Mary herself had taught me about getting information out of people. Usually, she said, if you stay quiet, people will keep talking to avoid the silence.

Unfortunately, Mary was wise to her own tricks. But I wasn't buying it. I hadn't imagined that scared look on her face or the phony perky attitude. She might be able to read people, but she couldn't act as well as Grace or Charlie.

"You don't seem it, that's all." I kept pushing. I knew I should drop it, but more than anything, I wanted Mary to know that if she was afraid, I was here for her, along with the rest of the team.

Mary sped up, moving in step beside me. "You know how I feel about this place," she admitted. "Every time I return to London, it reminds me. Of them."

My heart dropped. "Your parents," I said. I'd forgotten that Mary had lived in England for a brief time as a child, before her parents passed away. "I'm sorry."

She laughed easily. "It's fine, Nikki! You don't need to worry about me! Honestly, I think I'm a little freaked out about the whole virus thing," she said. A small flutter of relief appeared on her face, reddening her cheeks.

"Oh," I said, bowing my head. Who *wouldn't* be scared of a deadly virus?

"Well, that makes two of us." I decided to lighten the mood. "But, hey, you have to admit, some superhuman strength *would* be pretty awesome at times, right? Even if it's only temporary! Think of it, we could fight crime like the Avengers, with our muscly arms flexed for the world to see!" I flexed my arms playfully and made a face.

Mary giggled. "I don't know if I'd like wearing those tight leather pants they always make superheroes wear," she mused.

"True," I said. "I bet they're terrible in the summer. Think of the *sweat*!" I barked out a laugh, causing Grace to swivel her head around curiously behind her to see what all the noise was about.

"Right this way." A man at the entrance to the dark room that held the Crown Jewels beckoned us forward.

The first things I noticed were the luxurious navy blue walls. They gave the entire room a solemn, stuffy vibe and focused our attention on the main event.

"Whoa," Bert said. He shoved his glasses higher up on his nose, blinking in awe. "There they are! Billions of dollars worth of rocks and metal."

The jewels were artfully arranged in a glass display case, with lush red velvet pedestals beneath them. There were scepters, orbs, and glittering crowns studded with rubies, sapphires, and more diamonds than I'd ever seen, lit from all angles to show off every sparkle and flicker of light.

"Did you know that the oldest jewel here is over eight hundred years old?" Charlie babbled. She was talking up a storm, but it was all an act. Her feet moved artfully around the other tourists, navigating herself to the north side of the room with Leo.

"Nah," Leo said, winking at me. "It doesn't look a day over five hundred."

In case you're wondering, it is very difficult to look innocent when you're searching for suspicious people. Usually, you can busy yourself pretending to take pictures with your phone, but cameras aren't allowed in that room. Instead, we had to talk about the display in front of us like regular tourists, while still keeping a close watch on everybody else in the room.

"Do you see that diamond there?" Mary asked loudly enough to be mistaken for an obnoxious tourist. "The one in the middle of that purple crown?"

"Yeah," I said. "What about it?" I pretended to be super interested. It wasn't actually hard; billion-dollar diamonds two feet from your face are hard to ignore. Part of me wanted to break the glass and see if I could steal it, just because it was so shiny. Think of all the treats I could buy for Pickles with that kind of money!

"That's the Koh-i-Noor diamond," Mary said. Her eyes met mine briefly but then darted over my shoulder as she kept track of what was going on behind me. I followed her lead.

"It was supposedly first discovered in India, in the fifteenth century. It's one of the largest cut diamonds in the world. One hundred and five point six carats."

"That's one giant diamond. Wanna steal it?" I snickered.

Mary's eyes widened. "Don't make jokes like that around here! The Beefeaters take this stuff *very* seriously!"

"Why do they call 'em Beefeaters?" I glanced at the stern-faced guard by the door. "You'd think they should be protecting the world's most valuable T-bone."

The guard shook his head at my direction, his mouth pinching with annoyance. Clearly these guards couldn't take a joke.

"Oh, come on," I said, turning my attention back to the rest of the room, still searching for our suspect. "That rock would be a nice little souvenir from this *field trip* of ours . . ."

Mary grinned devilishly. "It's cursed, anyway, so you probably don't want it."

That got my attention. I shifted my weight on my hip and crossed my arms, still searching behind her. "For real?"

She nodded. "It's beautiful, right? And huge! Because of that, lots of people wanted it. It's surrounded by myth. Some say it was a gift to the earth from Surya, the sun god."

"That was nice of her," I mused, still scanning the room. Making quick eye contact with Grace across the room, I gave my head the tiniest of shakes while she did the same.

No sign of Victor anywhere.

"Others say it was stolen from the god Krishna while he was sleeping, and that it has magical powers," Mary continued. "Throughout history, it's been fought over, stolen, and lost repeatedly. It's now said that its owner will be granted power and the ability to rule the world, but that it will ultimately bring them only misfortune and death. And get this." Mary pointed to the diamond again. "It's only for *men*."

I turned back to her and rolled my eyes. "Of course it is. Sexist diamond."

"No, not the magical powers," Mary said. She crossed her arms over her chest. "The *curse*. While it jinxes all men who possess it, it's believed that the Koh-i-Noor diamond actually *protects* the women who wear it."

"Now that's a diamond I can get behind!" I said. "We should definitely lift it."

I thought Mary would laugh at my antics, but instead her mouth dropped open. A small lock of her hair had drifted over her face, but she didn't seem to notice. She was too busy staring at something—or someone—behind me.

I froze. "What is it?" I asked through gritted teeth. "Did you spot Victor?"

Refusing to blow our cover at such a crucial moment, I held my breath and shifted on my heel. Forcing myself to turn as slowly as possible, I prepared myself for trouble.

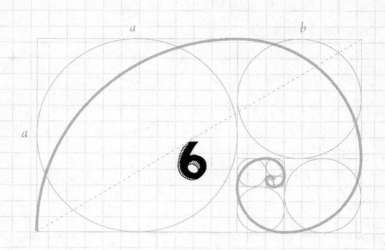

6

Mary's cheeks went pale, but she immediately shook her head, pulling herself back to the moment. "No," she said quickly. Her eyes narrowed, and she ducked her head slightly to the left, shifting to get a better view of something behind me. "It's just that . . . you know what? It's nothing."

I followed her gaze. Her weird, blank expression was hard to shake. "You look like you've seen a ghost, Mary."

I scanned the crowd for our suspicious-looking perp but found only young families, elderly retirees, and a few middle-aged women making their way out of the jewel room and back to the main hallway.

"I thought I saw someone I recognized, that's all!" Mary said, grabbing my shoulders and whirling me around. "Let's keep looking."

"Well, *who* was it, then?" I demanded. "You can't go all blank-faced like a robot and expect me not to notice." When I glanced in the direction she'd been looking, something caught my attention: a flash of brown hair, darting past a velvet rope that cordoned off an exit the Beefeaters weren't guarding.

Too fast, too out of place.

"Did you see that guy?" I took a step toward the spot where the man had been, waiting to see if he'd make another appearance. "He was alone. Brown hair and about the right height."

"Do you think it was Victor?" Mary glanced behind us.

I closed my eyes for a second, trying to remember the image I'd seen.

I hit the small transmitter above my ear. One of

my own audio-visual inventions—a GeckoDot—that allowed the team to communicate verbally and visually with one another while we were in the field. "Grace," I said. "I think it was him."

Mary stood taller, shifting on her feet. In each corner of the room, my friends all turned to face me.

"Where?" Grace's voice sounded loud and clear in my ear.

"He snuck out an off-limits exit; I'm not sure how he avoided the guard's attention. But we're not meant to go past that rope. And he did. Grace . . ." I clenched my fists. My desperation rose by the second. What if he got away before we could tag him? "He already has a head start. We need to go after him." I spoke through my teeth so the guards wouldn't hear me or read my lips. *"Now."*

Grace shook her head. "Whether or not he's ignoring visitor rules here, *we* can't be caught for doing the same. If we're caught, the mission fails. If we miss him, we miss him. We'll have to find him somewhere else. We should go outside to track him there."

Grace was right. And she *was* the team's leader. We all trusted her with our lives, and she'd never given me any reason to doubt her instincts. But something in my gut was telling me to follow the guy, anyway.

I huffed angrily and looked to the others for help.

Charlie, Bert, and Mo all stared grimly at me. And Mary was ever so slightly shaking her head in agreement with Grace. She even reached out like she might grab me if I made a move.

Anger rushed through me. "Guys, this isn't the time to be timid! The more I think about it, the more I *know* he matched the description. And he was acting suspicious, leaving from the other exit like that." I lowered my voice, but my urgent tone was bristly and sharp. "Please let me go after him. I can spray him while the rest of you distract the guards. There's no way he'll see me if the six of you do your jobs correctly."

I knew I was crossing a line with that last remark, but I swallowed down my guilt. Why didn't Grace understand? We were *this* close to finding Victor and might not get another chance.

"Sorry, Tesla," Grace said. She took a step toward me, but at that moment, another flash of black denim appeared in the corner of the room.

"That's *him*!" I hissed. The man had ducked through the door that he'd left a few seconds earlier. "Right there!" I balled my hands into fists and practically stomped my foot to get their attention. I wasn't exactly being casual, but I couldn't let Victor get away from us a second time.

Then something eerie happened. Almost as though he could sense me talking about him, the man turned and stared directly into my eyes.

My breath caught in my chest, and I jumped at the touch of Mary's fingers on my wrist. She'd seen the way he was looking at me, too.

"Stay put," Grace instructed. "I'm going over there."

I could feel my face turning hot. "No," I said. "You won't make it in time. He's onto us."

As the man started to duck behind the door again, he turned back to stare at me once more. He flashed the hint of a smile, then disappeared.

I jerked my head back in surprise.

This dude was toying with us!

I couldn't let him get away with it. It had to be a warning. If I didn't tag him today, I knew he'd be gone without a trace. He was smirking because he thought he had us beat already, that we couldn't stop him from selling Spark to the highest bidder or unleashing it on an unsuspecting public himself.

"I'm going after him," I said, and this time, I meant it.

Protests erupted in my ear. But I was already following my suspect as he wound his way through the tight stone corridors, away from the jewel room and the other tourists.

Behind me, a commotion began. It wasn't angry guards chasing after me; it was the raucous sounds of Mo and Charlie wailing. Even though I'd ignored Grace's orders, they were creating a distraction for me, anyway. I made a mental note to thank them, and the extra gratitude for my friends gave me the boost of energy I needed to move even faster.

"Wait!" The voice behind me caught me by surprise. Mary!

I reached my hand back to yank her toward me, hauling her along. "We've almost got him! He went this way." I ducked under a construction barrier and kept chasing Victor through the castle, willing my legs to move faster. The air got colder as we wound around damp hallways and corridors, bumping into walls worn with time. Quick

flashes of his black jacket and shoes were enough to tell me that we were catching up.

A smile grew on my face as we raced up a stone staircase. "He's running out of places to go," I panted. "We've almost got him. Get ready!"

Mary let out a scared whimper behind me but kept pace.

Following the man around a final corner, I skidded to a stop. Dust clogged the air, and there was a distinct smell of mold and damp earth.

"Where'd he go?!" Mary asked. She whipped her head around, checking the small window slits for any sign of him.

It was like walking a plank. One minute, I had steady ground beneath me, the next, my stomach plummeted.

My suspect was *gone*.

"He was right here!" I shouted, gripping the small canister of aerosolized tracker paint that Martha had left each of us. "There's literally nowhere else he could have gone! How did we lose him?!"

Mary wiped the sweat from her forehead with her sleeve. "Maybe he took a quick turn we didn't see? Or..." Her voice trailed off. She looked to the tiny windows.

"No." I shook my head. "There's no way he jumped out there."

"Grace," Mary called over her GeckoDot. "He's not here."

My hand whipped to my ear when Grace didn't answer, sending my stomach sinking with disappointment once again. My own GeckoDot must have fallen off while I was running, but Mary was still able to communicate with the team.

"Uh-huh," Mary said, answering Grace. "No. Completely gone."

Mary's mouth tightened into a thin line. Whatever Grace was saying, I was glad I couldn't hear it for once. It wasn't the first time I'd disobeyed her orders, but this time definitely felt like the worst.

And I hadn't even successfully tagged my suspect to make up for it.

I pored over every inch of the room, desperate for a small closet, trunk, or anywhere the man could have hidden. But there was nothing.

"It's fine," Mary said, still talking to the others. "We'll meet you all outside. Yes, I know." Mary stared at me. They were talking about me now. "No, she's okay, too. I'll tell her. Wait . . ."

The abrupt change in Mary's tone made me twitch. I

picked myself up from where I was inspecting the floor for a secret exit and looked at her.

She stood ramrod straight, with her arm outstretched and pointed toward the window.

"There's something here . . ." Her voice was barely a whisper.

I crept over to where she was pointing. How had I missed the small black candle, flickering on the narrow windowsill?

Peering at the candle more closely, disappointment swept over me. It wasn't the only thing I'd missed. A small, folded piece of paper sat tucked on its side against the window. Easily overlooked, if not for the candle acting as a beacon.

"It's a note," Mary repeated to the others. "Hang on. Nikki, be *careful*."

I took my time picking the note up from the ledge, ensuring there were no traps or hidden mechanisms. But it was a regular piece of paper. A stamped glob of black wax sealed the note shut. Some sort of lightning-shaped pattern stared back at me.

Taking care not to damage the image, I carefully pried the note open, lifting the wax in one piece.

"She's reading it." Mary continued to narrate my movements for the others.

I'd already been twitching with exertion from our chase, but the minute I began to read the note, a whole new set of tremors started to build in my body.

"We've got a problem," I croaked. A sharp pain stabbed my chest, right above my heart. Handing the note to Mary, I wished I could go back in time— back to the jewel room, back to Costa Rica, *anywhere* that wasn't here, where my entire team was in immediate danger.

Mary read the note. She exhaled slowly, with one long shaky breath. "Grace." She blinked at me, shaking her head. "You need to get out of there as fast as you can."

I could hear vague mumbling coming from the others from Mary's GeckoDot. They were demanding answers before they left in a hurry.

"Just do it!" Mary screamed. "It's a setup! *GET OUT NOW!*"

But it was too late. The sudden rumble beneath our feet made the mortar and dust from the stones above us crumble over our heads, like floating ash from a volcano.

"Was that an explosion?!" I gasped, gripping Mary's arm tight. My bones seemed to shake inside my body with the force of the blast. "Are they okay?!"

Mary snatched the note from me and held it to the

light, scrutinizing it like it might suddenly catch fire. The taunting words were still etched into my mind. Words I never thought I'd see after chasing a random stranger through an ancient castle in London. Words written by someone who had just blown up the Tower of London.

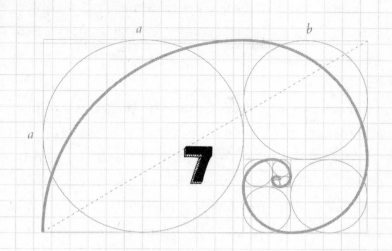

There was no time for questions. Three things were clear to me:

1. The man I'd chased through the Tower had left us the note. There wasn't a doubt in my mind that he'd known we were going to be here today looking for him.
2. Whoever he was, he'd somehow managed to set off a bomb in the Tower of London.
3. Worst of all: I'd really messed up.

No, "messed up" didn't cover it. I'd completely and utterly failed in what felt like the most colossal way possible.

Mary and I managed to follow a smoky trail of corridors back to the grounds of the castle, where we were hoping beyond hope to meet the others in one piece.

But when we erupted from the building, coughing and shaking, our friends were nowhere to be seen.

Mary rushed over to a guard who stood on alert by one of the doorways. Crowds of tourists were still being evacuated from the building, but since no one was allowed to leave the premises, we were surrounded by a confused, disoriented crowd.

"Please help us!" Mary told the guard. "We're looking for our friends! They were in the jewel room—did everyone get out okay?"

The guard glowered at Mary, then looked past her shoulder to stare at me. A glimmer of recognition crossed his face.

Shoot.

"Mary!" I hissed. I grabbed her hand to pull her away. "We'll find them ourselves—we should go!"

That's when a pair of vises gripped my shoulders, cementing me to the spot. No, not vises. *Hands.*

"Nikola Tesla?" My captor forced me to turn and face him head-on. His cheekbones sliced sharp corners on his face. Between that and his muscled frame, he looked like he was made of granite. Despite the commotion around us and the dust still floating in the air, there wasn't a speck or wrinkle on his gray suit.

"Um," I started. "No?"

He scoffed at me. That's when I heard the three words nobody ever wants to hear when their friends have possibly been killed in a horrible explosion in a foreign country.

"You're under arrest."

"What?!" Mary gaped at him. "You can't arrest her! You think we had something to do with the explosion? We're looking for our friends!"

To my surprise, Mary began hitting the man's thick forearms with her fists. Clearly she needed to spend some more time in the Academy gym, because he didn't even blink. Instead, he gestured to one of his uniformed colleagues with a flick of his chin.

"And there's the Shelley girl," he said. "Arrest her, as well."

Now it was my turn to protest. "Hey!" I shouted, using the man's weight to hold me up while I lifted my feet from the ground and kicked at the other officer. "Leave her alone!"

I should have been embarrassed to be making a scene like that in front of a huge crowd of tourists. After all, I probably looked like some horrible brat who'd been caught red-handed destroying a national monument. But couldn't they see that beneath my snarky exterior beat the heart of do-gooder?

"That's enough!" the man who held me yelled in my ear, wrenching my arms so my feet landed back on the ground with a thud. "You're both coming with us."

"What, exactly, do you think we *did*?" I demanded, still desperate to free myself from his grip as he led me to a small squad car by the entrance of the castle grounds. To my dismay, it wasn't a local police car. If they weren't cops, who were they?! I started to kick again, clumsily hoisting myself against his shoulder.

"We're being kidnapped!" I screamed as loud as I possibly could, trying to get the crowd's attention. *"Help us!"* I twisted again, and this time managed to catch my abductor in the kneecap.

"Watch it!" he bellowed. "Oi, kid! Relax! I'm a British Intelligence agent!" He stopped dragging me long enough to produce a badge from his wallet, practically stuffing it up my nose.

You'd think I'd be slightly relieved that I wasn't being manhandled by regular, run-of-the-mill attackers. But out of the two options, my chances of escape were significantly lower with these trained agents.

There was only one course of action: talk my way out of trouble. Whatever they thought we did—it was nonsense. "Why are we being arrested? You have to tell us."

"You know bloody well why we're bringing you in," the agent said. He shoved me toward his car. My sneakers caught on the cobblestone, nearly sending me tumbling to my knees.

I craned my neck to stare him down, aiming for my most sarcastic tone. "If you'd just *listen*, you'd know that my friends and I are trying to *protect* people!"

"We'll sort out just exactly what you've been up to at headquarters, *Nikola*." He drew out my name like a curse. Then he cupped the back of my head with one hand and opened the back door of his car with the other. "In you go."

The swagger on his face was easy to read as he sank into the driver's seat and turned to face Mary and me. "We know exactly who you are. Both of you."

"I doubt it," Mary quipped. "That information is top secret."

I couldn't help but grin at her attitude. Apparently getting arrested was all she needed to let out a little bit of snark.

"Oh, is it?" The agent asked. "Nikola Tesla. Mary Shelley. And we already have your five friends in custody. You're Genius Academy kids, and you've been running around the world causing trouble. But this time, you've gone too far. *That's* why we're arresting you."

I rolled my eyes but had to force a nervous glance at Mary. How did this guy know about Genius Academy? And more importantly, if he knew about our school, why was he treating us like criminals? We tried to protect the world not harm it.

"You're arresting us because you think we blew up some fancy jewels?" I barked at him.

He wrapped his hand around the steering wheel and shifted the car into drive, sending Mary and me lurching back in our seats. "No," he said. "We're not arresting you for blowing them up. We're arresting you for stealing them."

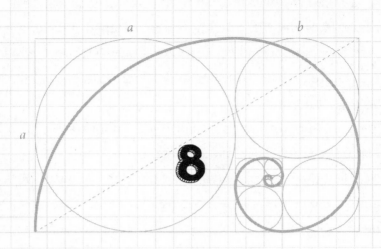

I'm not sure what it is about traveling abroad that always lands me in police custody.

Is it that foreign law enforcement officers don't like the look of me? Did I steal candy from babies in a previous life, or laugh at tiny puppies who couldn't climb up the stairs on their own? This could be karma's way of settling the score. Or maybe—just maybe—I've got horrible luck because I hang out with certified geniuses who get into trouble for a living.

Whatever the reason, I didn't care. My only priority was getting out of that stupid interrogation room so I could make sure my friends were okay. Even Pickles, who had been with Charlie in the Tower, was missing. Had she gotten caught in the explosion as well? I needed *answers*, but the MI6 agent staring me down wasn't exactly keen on letting me out of his sight.

"My name is Agent Donnelly. We can do this the easy way, or we can do this the hard way." He loosened his gray tie and shifted his collar. Judging by the beads of sweat at his hairline and his reddened cheeks, he was overheating in this muggy room even more than I was.

SPECIAL AGENT PICKLES
MISSING IN ACTION

"Seriously?" I let my hands drop loudly to the arms of the metal chair, which clattered against the cuffs on my wrists. "You guys actually *say* stuff like that? Look, this is all a huge misunderstanding. My friends and I didn't have anything to do with that explosion."

A small grin of triumph appeared on his face. "It could have been an earthquake, you know. Construction, even. But you're certain it was an explosion. Seems to me like you know much more than you're letting on, Nikola."

I couldn't believe this guy. "Oh please! An earthquake?! You know as well as I do that an earthquake wouldn't only impact the Tower, duh."

It was his turn to gawk at me. "Now you're an expert on earthquakes, are you?"

He was getting more arrogant by the second. Why wouldn't anyone *listen* to me?!

I took a deep breath. "I know that in 2015, there was a four-point-two magnitude earthquake that hit Kent. And that the strongest known earthquake to hit the UK was in 1931, near the Dogger Bank. And I know that the earthquakes here rarely do any damage. Especially not damage that results in a massive evacuation of one of London's biggest paid tourist attractions. So between that and your ridiculous construction theory, there is really only one other option, so *arewedonehereyet?*"

That got his attention.

"You know why I don't like you kids?" His lip curled in annoyance, sending my stomach twisting. All I'd done was anger him further.

"I guess you're going to tell me." I shifted awkwardly in my metal chair.

"Because you *interfere*." He pointed a long finger at my face, and a muscle in his jaw jumped. "Wherever there's trouble, I don't have to look very hard to find evidence that you kids have been there. Thinking you're *saving the world* when you should be staying out of the way and letting grown-ups do their jobs."

I licked my cracked lips. "Maybe if you so-called *grown-ups* would actually do some of the world-saving yourselves, then we wouldn't have to," I sneered. "You think we want to do all the dirty work for you?"

If Grace were here, she'd give me a look and tell me to chill out and hold my tongue. But she wasn't—none of my team was—and until I found out where they were being held, I couldn't help being more reckless than normal.

"And what work is that?" Agent Donnelly asked. "Stealing a priceless diamond?"

"You think I could steal the Crown Jewels from one of the most highly secure vaults on the planet?" I asked incredulously. I mean, there were approximately seventy-seven flaws in the Tower security system, but he didn't *need* to know that.

"You tell me," he said.

"I'm *telling* you," I said through gritted teeth. "You're making a mistake here. We're on the same side."

"We'll see about that," he said. "First, you've got a visitor. But don't get too excited. We're only giving her a chance to speak to you as part of a deal." He was trying to act casual, but I could tell by the way his chest puffed up that he was proud of whatever he'd gotten out of the arrangement.

"Who?" I asked. My thoughts raced. Everyone I knew had already been arrested or was on another continent.

He nodded his head slightly, gesturing to someone behind the metal door. "Bring her in," he instructed.

I heard a sharp knock, followed by a metallic creak. As the door opened, the first thing I saw was the shiny black leather of her shoes, reflecting the fluorescent light. Her hair was frazzled, and her usually smooth complexion was dotted with a sheen of sweat. But she appeared to be unharmed.

"Martha!" My voice cracked, and instantly a huge weight of anxiety and fear lifted from my chest. Agent Donnelly clamped his huge hand on my shoulder as I rose, catching me by surprise. My head jerked back and slammed him near the temple.

"Oops." I glared at him.

"Stay put," he barked, rubbing his eye.

Like I had a choice with these handcuffs.

I sat taller in my chair and fought the giddiness in my chest.

You guys are in trouble now! I practically beamed at Agent Donnelly. We were *all* going to get out of here.

I expected to hear Martha's calm, measured voice tell me that everything was going to be all right. That she had already arranged for our release. We'd be on our way back to the Academy within the hour.

Unfortunately, that is *not* what I got.

"Nikola Tesla," she said. Her voice was low but sharp as glass. A small vein in her forehead that I'd never noticed before throbbed angrily.

"M-Martha?" My cheeks were hot, and my stomach plummeted. Her tone was all wrong. The anger emanating from her was palpable.

"Don't you *Martha* me!" She barked, causing me to wince in surprise. "Do you have any idea how much trouble you're all in?! You're going to return that diamond," she said, slamming her hand on the table with each word. "*Right. This. Minute!*"

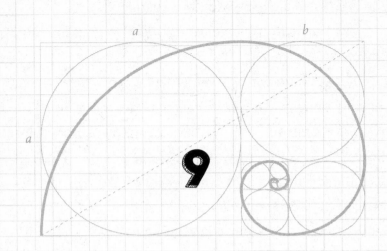

9

I stared in shock at the faint dents that Martha left on the metal table.

"Wait." I held up my hands in protest. The handcuffs felt tighter than ever, and Agent Donnelly's stares were practically burning a hole in the back of my head. "Stop joking around, Martha! This guy actually thinks we stole that stupid diamond—you're making it worse! This isn't funny!"

"It's over, kid," Agent Donnelly interrupted, stepping between Martha and I. "We've got you on surveillance *talking* about stealing the Koh-i-Noor with your little friend. You and the Shelley girl exited, two of your buddies created a diversion, the bomb blew up outside the room, and somehow in the commotion the other three broke the display and made off with the diamond. It's all on camera. We need you to tell us where they stashed the diamond."

"It was a *joke!*" I spat. "We weren't there to steal a diamond! We were there to track down a criminal on Martha's orders!" I jabbed my finger in the air and pointed to her. "Ask her. Martha, please tell him!"

"I will *not* lie to a member of MI6, young lady!" Martha's voice rose dangerously, sending my heart into a tailspin. Why was she doing this? Had Martha set us up? What was I missing?!

Also: *young lady*?! It was one thing to throw me to the wolves in a foreign country, but calling me "young lady" like I was some bratty child who refused to go to bed on time? That was going too far.

I had to try another tactic, so I turned my attention back to Agent Donnelly. "You've got me talking about stealing the diamond, *and* you've got the others actually stealing it? Is that right?"

Agent Donnelly's shoulders tensed. "We have more than enough to arrest you, Nikola," he said.

"Ha!" I dragged my chair back against the wall. I had no idea how to get out of this room, but I wouldn't give him the satisfaction of thinking he'd proven anything. "So you *don't* have any of us on camera actually stealing it!"

"The explosion knocked out the surveillance at that particular point in time . . ." he said.

"Uh-huh." I laughed. "*Suuuure.* And that's perfect, isn't it? You guys don't have the evidence, so you decide to pick us up so you can look like you know what you're doing!"

"*ENOUGH!*" Martha's voice boomed, sending a shock up my spine and straight down to my toes. She shifted between Agent Donnelly and me, blocking him from view. I tried to skid away from her, but the hard concrete wall bashed against my shoulder. I still couldn't figure out why she was lying about us. Had she hit her head? Was she being coerced? Was she a double agent who had made off with the diamond herself?

Martha leaned down, her nose within inches of mine as she spoke. "Ms. Tesla, you listen and listen good."

I shrank down at her vicious tone. Martha or not—she still had the ability to scare the wits out of me with her calm fury.

"I've had it up to here with your antics," she said. "*All of you!* How am I expected to do *my* job if I'm stuck covering up all your messes!"

My lip trembled, but I willed myself not to cry. "Why are you doing this to us?"

I couldn't believe she thought so little of us. We got

into trouble, sure. But we did our best, and it wasn't our fault that evil people were out to destroy the world on a regular basis. It wasn't our fault we weren't *perfect* at saving the day—we're kids!

I winced as Martha reached toward me and gripped my shoulders in her hands.

"You're in the way, Nikki. Sometimes complicated problems require elementary solutions, and what the world needs now is for you and the others to stay out of trouble."

"Step back, ma'am," Agent Donnelly warned her.

My insides twisted as Martha released my shoulders, but something about her expression gave me pause. A twinkle of mystery as her gaze drifted from my eyes down to my right shoulder.

"Watch your back, Nikki," she said.

And then the tiniest hint of a smile appeared on her face, followed by a blink of her eye.

No, not a blink. A *wink*.

The realization hit me at once. *She was still on my side.*

Instantly, my priorities shifted. What was she planning? What was I supposed to do? I wanted nothing more than to show her that I understood,

Unfortunately, I didn't have the chance, because at that moment, Agent Donnelly grabbed her by the arm and began dragging her from the room. "That's all you get," he said. "I promised you five minutes. We'll deal with the kids from here."

Martha didn't struggle, but I had to on her behalf. "No!" I said, leaping up. "Where are you taking her?"

Agent Donnelly pursed his lips together. "Some genius you are," he said dismissively. "I already told you. Martha's giving us everything she knows about you and your little mission to steal that diamond, and in return, we're going to lessen her sentence. That's how it works in the real world."

"Her *sentence*?!" I cried, reaching toward them. "You can't do that! Leave her alone!"

"Stop, Nikki," Martha said, glaring angrily back at me. "You've done more than enough. Remember what I said. *Watch your back.*" She turned to Agent Donnelly imploringly. "And would you please get her something to drink? She's going to pass out in this heat without water. You should know better."

The door slammed behind them, leaving me under the buzzing spotlight. The sweat on my back and streaks of tears along my cheeks made me feel clammy and anxious.

Whatever Martha was warning me about, I'd have to face it alone.

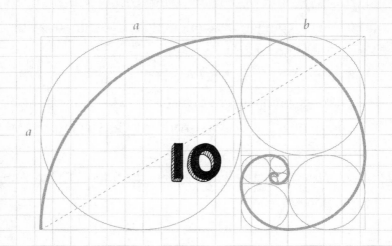

10

Okay, deep breath.

I was on my own, but with Martha still on our side, there *had* to be a way out of this predicament.

What had she said again? She'd told me that I belonged at home. Out of the way. There had to be more to her message than that. Going *home* wouldn't help anyone right now, and besides, all our families were scattered across the country.

Unless . . .

Our home was the Academy itself. Was she telling me to go back to the Academy? But that was so far away from Victor and his serum. Going back to school meant giving up on this mission, and she wouldn't want us to do that.

"Home," I whispered to myself. I pictured all the homes she could be talking about. Homes with families. Homes with friends. Homes with safety . . .

That's it.

The Genius Academy safe house in London! Back in Costa Rica, Martha had told us to go there if we ran into trouble. It was the one place we had in this town that could keep us safe.

She wanted me to escape.

But how on earth was I supposed to do that? Martha couldn't even escape herself, so what were *my* chances?

Watch your back, Nikki.

My hand twitched instinctively.

She hadn't just left me with one message. She'd left me with two. Could she have meant that literally? I could still practically feel the squeeze of her hands on my shoulders . . .

Sitting taller in my chair, I craned my torso to the side, scooting my butt forward as I leaned my back against my left hand. The handcuffs dug into my wrist as I groped around the middle of my back with the back of my hand.

Hair. Shirt. Fuzzball.

There!

My fingers clamped around a small hard object attached to the back of my shirt. Martha must have stuck it there when she'd grabbed me. I edged back up in my chair to a normal sitting position to examine my find. Was it the key to my handcuffs? A secret weapon that would thwart my captors?

Fat chance.

"A hair clip?" I muttered. "Seriously, Martha?"

That's right. She'd left me a secret weapon all right, but it wasn't one I was expecting. I turned the small metal hair clip over carefully in my hand. If she'd left it with me, it was sure to be no ordinary hair clip. Was it a transmitter or a communicator? Right now, that didn't matter to me. Instead I focused on the small metal prongs that formed the thinnest part of the clip. Holding the back firmly with three fingers, I pried the metal away from the rest of the clip. Maybe I didn't need a key, after all. The prongs were thin enough, but would they do the trick?

I groaned with pain as I forced my hand to twist awkwardly so I could shove the metal prongs into the tiny hole in my handcuff. Then I began to jiggle them as if my life depended on it.

Almost.

Almost . . .

There!

I sucked in a deep breath and turned to make sure nobody had seen anything. Surveillance cameras were on me, but I could only hope that the guards who were supposed to monitor them were on a coffee break or didn't think I was important enough to watch at all times.

With one hand free, it was easy getting my other hand out of the cuff.

"Thank you, Martha," I breathed.

One step down.

Now how was I going to get out of this room—this *building*—without anyone noticing? Keeping my hands positioned on the arms of the chair in case anyone was looking, I aimlessly turned the mangled metal hair clip in my hand, searching my mind for a possible solution.

That's when I saw it. A small pink flash, smiling up at me from the underside of the clip.

"What the . . . ?" A tiny vial of pink liquid was held there by a thin line of transparent glue.

Pulling the vial free, I stuck the clip back in my hair, in case Agent Donnelly returned. Lifting the vial to my nose, I took a sniff and was instantly hit with a wave of sharp nausea.

Whatever was in the vial, it sure didn't smell good.

"Okay, Martha," I whispered to myself. "What am I supposed to do with this?"

I rattled through the list of possibilities in my head. There wasn't much liquid—less than half a teaspoon. Was it reactive? Maybe if I threw it on the ground, it'd

explode like Martha's cartridges and cause a distraction so I could make my escape. Or maybe it'd just catch fire and kill us all.

That would be counterproductive.

Was I meant to pour it inside the lock on the door? Or in Agent's Donnelly's drink? None of my options really jumped out at me. How on earth was I supposed to get out of here with nothing but this pink stuff?

I licked my lips, the dry grit of my tongue like sandpaper. Martha was right—I *was* dehydrated. I looked to the locked door, suddenly picturing Agent Donnelly returning with that glass of water Martha had mentioned.

And then her words came back to me: "*Would you please get her something to drink?*"

I stared forward, battling the voice in my head.

That's what she wanted me to do. The metal hair clip had been a message, but she hadn't wasted a word either.

I wasn't supposed to throw the vial, or use it against Agent Donnelly.

Martha wanted me to drink it.

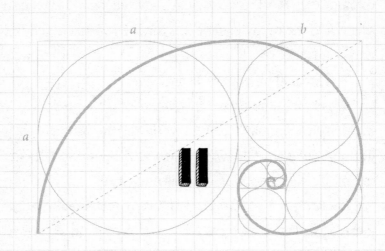

With desperate fingers, I removed the teensy plastic cap from the vial, taking another quick smell of the pink liquid inside. Was it possible I'd misunderstood her clues? I hoped I wasn't about to drink poison. But while I wasn't sure what exactly this stuff would do to me, I had to take the chance. I couldn't sit here like a lump, waiting for Agent Donnelly to return and lock me up for good.

Even action you're not sure about is better than zero action, right?

"This better work," I muttered to myself. Before I could chicken out, I lifted the vial to my lips and tipped it back, draining the liquid onto my tongue.

I swallowed the mouthful and shuddered at the tart,

metallic flavor. *"Echh!"* I smacked my lips loudly and shook my head. The taste was even worse than the smell—like spaghetti sauce with a side of rotten banana. What the heck was in that stuff?

Breathing slowly and deliberately, I waited for something amazing to happen. Come on, superpowers! Come on, shrinking ability! Come on, magic potion from Martha!

Unfortunately, the only sensation I felt was a gurgle in my stomach. A *loud* gurgle.

"Oh, *ew*," I said, clutching my abdomen.

I must have spectacular timing, because Agent Donnelly stepped back into the room while I was doubled over, cursing Martha. Whatever I'd drunk, it must've been expired, because the only thing it'd given me was the urgent need for a restroom.

Signs You Are About to Lose Your Lunch

can't fight tears

spasming stomach

face looks green

mouth full of noxious mystery poison

"Whoa," Agent Donnelly exclaimed. "What happened here? What did you do? And who let you out of your cuffs?"

I continued to grab my stomach while tears streamed from my eyes. They weren't from sadness; they were from strain. I was about four seconds away from losing my lunch all over the table.

"Someone... another agent came in... I... I don't know!" I cried, hoping my lie was convincing. I couldn't explain the cuffs, but at that point, all I could think about was that I really *had* just swallowed poison.

I was getting more scared by the second, and I knew it must have showed on my face because Agent Donnelly looked seriously worried.

"Can I go to the bathroom? *Please?!*" I begged. "I'm gonna..." I stopped short, gagging on my words. My hand whipped over my mouth to prevent the worst from happening.

Oh God, why did I drink that stuff?!

Agent Donnelly hesitated. I knew he'd be wondering if this was some sort of ploy for me to get out of this room. But honestly, I was feeling pretty lucky right now to be *upright*, and escape was the last thing on my mind.

"Kid, you're *green*," he said. He stooped over to help lift me from my near-fetal position on the chair. "Come on, let's get you sorted out. Don't try anything though, okay?"

If he didn't believe me before, the fact that I clutched onto him desperately with clammy hands as we shuffled to the bathroom down the hall probably helped.

"Wait a second," he instructed. He grabbed an extra set of handcuffs and gripped my wrists, locking them into place with a solid click. "I'll be waiting right here," he said, holding the door open for me.

"Mmhphhf," I answered, still trying to hold in my breakfast. If I hadn't been so worried about puking all over him, I'd probably have cared more about the cuffs. But right now? I needed a toilet, and fast!

I barely noticed my surroundings as I lurched toward a stall.

"Acckkk," I cried, clutching my roiling stomach. "Martha, *whyyy?"*

After a couple of long, disgustingly memorable minutes, my stomach started to return to normal, and my frantic heart began to settle back to a normal rhythm. I tore some toilet paper from the roll and wiped my mouth. Now that the horrible pink stuff was gone from my system, my head began to clear. I shifted on my knees and leaned against the side of the stall.

How could I have misread Martha's signals so badly?

Taking a deep breath, I forced myself to stand, rolled my tight shoulders back, and braced myself for the inevitable pang of returning tummy trouble, but it never came.

"Huh," I said aloud. I wiped my mouth with another ribbon of toilet paper.

In fact, I felt ridiculously fine for someone who'd poisoned herself on purpose. Was it possible . . . ?

Hauling myself to the spotless mirror by the sink, I tilted my head and stared at my reflection. I could practically see Martha in the mirror, giving me that knowing glance, her eyebrow slightly quirked.

Think, Tesla. Use your brain.

Maybe I hadn't misread her signals at all.

The sink reflected the bright fluorescent lights above me, reminding me of the sun. It had to be setting outside by now, near twilight.

Martha had said out loud that I needed a drink. And planted the vial in the hairclip. I caught my expression in the mirror once more.

There was no way of escaping the building from that tiny locked room Agent Donnelly was keeping me in. But Martha had given me a way out of *that* particular room.

Now I was alone in what had to be a much less secure room—with no surveillance and no guards in sight.

That meant that the way out of the building was in this room.

Agent Donnelly knocked lightly on the door. "Everything all right in there, Nikki?"

I sucked in a breath, jumping at his voice. "Yes!" I made myself sound as croaky and ill as possible. "I'm sorry, I'll be right out!" I kept it up with a few more puking sounds and jumped back in the stall to flush the toilet again.

Then I got to work.

There were two high-set windows in the restroom, and a look outside told me that we were well above the first floor. Probably more like the fourth or fifth. But if Martha had directed me here with the barfing juice, there *had* to be roof access. If I could get out a window, maybe I could make a run for it before Agent Donnelly knew what hit him.

But . . .

My hands reflexively tugged against the handcuffs. *These stupid things!* There was no way Donnelly would let me out of his sight without them on. Luckily, I still had my handy hair clip tucked in my—

What?! No!

I cupped my hands over my whole head, searching desperately for the clip. It must have fallen out somewhere in the hallway while Agent Donnelly helped me limp to the bathroom. My stomach turned again, but this time it was from my own stupidity.

But I couldn't let something as mundane as handcuffs stop me from escaping. *Keep moving, Tesla.*

Bolting from stall to stall, I began to inspect everything: the toilets, the paper holder, the garbage slots. Martha was all about backup plans. There was a chance that Agent Donnelly would have confiscated the clip anyway. She had to have hidden a key *somewhere* in here for me. While I was searching, I threw out the odd cough and gag, so Agent Donnelly would think I was still sick.

I flushed a random toilet again and stood back. Drumming my fingers together, I could feel that I was right about the key but clearly wrong about where she'd hidden it.

"Come on, Martha . . ." I whispered. "Help me out one more time." I replayed every single interaction we'd had since this awful mission had begun.

"Nikola?" Agent Donnelly called out again. The only reason he wasn't barging in yet was because he thought I was contained. I had to keep him believing that.

"Just getting some water!" I yelped. "I'm still here!"

Get her a drink.

There it was. It was like Martha was talking in my head now, which was equal parts scary and awesome.

There was only one place to get a drink in this restroom. Once again, Martha had given me many clues in one simple sentence. She hadn't only been talking about the vial, after all.

Turning back to the sink, I knew exactly where to look. The faucets were motion-activated, which meant nobody ever really had to touch them. Craning my neck and poring over each one with my fingers, I nearly leaped for joy when I felt the small metallic key.

"I'll be right out!" I yelled. "I'm feeling a little better. I think it's almost out of my system!"

Oops. I should have sounded sicker when I said that.

"Hurry up," Agent Donnelly's patience was quickly waning.

I let out another fake barf noise and started running the faucet in the sink. Agent Donnelly would think I was washing my hands, but what I was really doing was disguising any clinking sounds the handcuffs were making as I twisted my arms into a pretzel to get the stupid things off me.

"Coming! Coming!" I swiped my hand under the hand dryer, setting it off. Grateful for the incredibly loud whooshing that rushed from it, I used the sound as a cover to take a running start at the wall with the window, hurling myself up to grip the sill and yank it open.

Would you believe MI6 doesn't lock their windows?

That was a big mistake. Huge.

Seconds before I hurled myself out of the building, a brief moment of hesitation stopped me short. I didn't want to leave the others behind, but no matter how I worked the equations in my  head, there was no way to help them escape that didn't end with me back in those cuffs. And Martha had given me pretty clear instructions, hadn't she?

I was to regroup at the safe house first, then find a way to help them get out of here.

I tucked my sweatshirt hood over my head and popped the collar of my jacket up to brace against the growing chill in the air.

"Two Twenty-One B, Baker Street." I said the safe house address aloud to myself as I peered down at the rooftop below. Beyond that, the skyline of London was waiting for me. "Go."

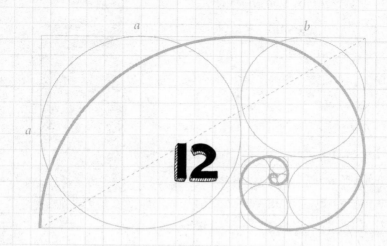

If you've never been unlucky enough to need a place to hide from the secret service in a foreign country, let me say this: It is not as glamorous as it sounds. In every movie I'd seen, the good guys always showed up at a mysterious—not to mention luxurious—untraceable home where a collection of passports, wigs, colored contacts, and various gadgets and technological wonders waited for them.

But when I picked the lock of the safe house on Baker Street, all I got were spiders. There were webs hanging from the corners of the front door, along the mail slot, and all over the welcome mat, like outdated Halloween decorations.

Oh, and one more thing . . .

"What took you so long?"

The makeshift lock pick I'd scavenged from the garbage bins outside clattered to the floor.

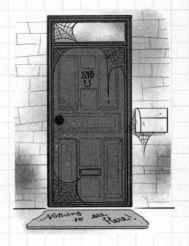

Here's the thing: I'd spent the entire journey to the safe house feeling guilty. Like, overwhelmingly, gut-wrenchingly guilty. I'd left all my friends behind to fend for themselves, in the clutches of an organization that hated them and wanted to lock them up for the rest of their lives. Every step on my way to the safe house, I was devising how I'd find a way to break them out.

Little did I know, it was all a wasted effort.

Because my team wasn't handcuffed and desperate, tears rolling down their cheeks while they pleaded for help.

They were in front of me, with bowls of macaroni and cheese on their laps, leisurely watching the nightly news.

All six of them. Even Pickles was sprawled out on the floor in front of Charlie's feet, with her own bowl of food. A goopy mustache of melted cheese covered her snout.

"Wait." I held up a hand. The scene in front of me

began to sink in. I bent over to snatch my lock pick. "I'm the *last* one here? Seriously?" I let my shoulders drop with annoyance. "I spent the last hour trying to figure out how to help you all escape!"

"Well, that was awfully kind of you," Bert said, his smile beaming widely. There was a chunk of noodle stuck to his lower lip. "But we had it covered!"

I plunked down on a musty chair, batting away the cloud of dust that erupted under my nose.

I suppose I should have known. My friends had been in the world-saving business for longer than I had, so it made sense they'd all be master escape artists by now. But *still*. Why did I have to be the last one? I slid down in my chair, trying to hide my disappointment. "How did you all get here so quickly?"

Leo spoke first, arcing a bottle of fruit punch through the air toward me. "Charlie and I got away before the car actually made it to MI6 headquarters," he explained. "We've been here for hours. That's why we made dinner for everyone." He held up his bowl in celebration. "To freedom!"

Bert laughed, lifting his forkful of noodles to salute Leo. "To *cheese* and freedom!"

"And how did you get out, Einstein?" I asked him, crossing my arms over my chest. I was starving, and the macaroni and cheese *did* smell delicious, but I was too miffed to feel like celebrating yet.

Bert set his fork down. "You know, Nikki. Sometimes you really need to use your *brains* to escape a situation . . ."

"We set off a stink bomb and escaped through the air ducts," Mo said flatly.

I sniffed the air dramatically. "I thought I smelled something off in here." I looked back to Bert, who was thoroughly annoyed that Mo had spilled the beans about their escape. "Some brains you've got there. No wonder you reek."

I turned to Mary. She was the only one with the decency to look guilty.

"Sorry, Nikki. We wanted to go back and get you,

too, but Martha gave us strict instructions. Any attempts to coordinate our escapes would have meant risking them entirely. She trusted you'd get out okay. You know we'd have helped you if you hadn't made it out tonight on your own."

"I escaped *fine!*" I said, more to myself than anyone else. "How did you get out?"

"The agent who was interrogating me has three daughters," she said, like that answered my question. "I asked if I could make a phone call to my mother, and he let me. He should *not* have. It was only a bobby pin and a couple of rooms away from the exit."

A smirk crossed my face. "Are you telling me you manipulated him into feeling sorry for you? Using the love of his daughters to play him like a fiddle?"

"Yes," she said. "Yes I am. And it worked." She took another big bite of her dinner and pet Pickles with the tip of her toe.

"All right, Grace. Let's hear it." I asked. Grace was chewing her mac and cheese quietly, surveying the rest of us.

Shrugging, she lifted her chin defiantly. "Me? I asked nicely."

I scoffed. Marching over to the kitchen island, I helped myself to the bowl of pasta that was waiting for me. "Well, that's all *fantastic*." I shoveled a mouthful of food into my face and sat back down angrily. "So I was the only one who had to *poison* myself, huh? That was awfully nice of Martha." I swallowed down the bitter taste of resentment. It did not pair well with cheese, let me tell you.

"Yikes," Charlie said. "Did you really barf all over?"

I nodded.

"At least we're all safe here, and together again," Mary said. She walked over to give me a quick hug. "We've got food and laptops . . . We can continue the mission from here."

Mo's large shoulders drooped. "I was kind of hoping for a chance to shower first," he admitted. "I still smell like skunk." He glanced at Bert, who plugged his nose with two fingers.

"It's true," he said. "Mo caught the worst of the stink bomb."

"Yeah." Mo glared at Bert. "Funny how you managed to keep *yourself* mostly out of range when you threw it, huh?" He gripped his fork in one hand and flicked a noodle at Bert. It landed directly on his glasses.

Ignoring the droopy macaroni, Bert continued. "There's also some good news." He smiled proudly, reached down beside his chair, and lifted a small laptop with one hand. "I've got information on Victor."

I perked up. With all the handcuffs, escaping, and barfing, I'd almost forgotten what had brought us to England in the first place.

"Martha gave me a coded message while we were in custody," he said. "Leo and I deciphered it and found coordinates that led to—"

"Wait!" Mo hissed. He jumped up from his chair, faster than I'd ever seen him move before. Then he held his hand up to silence us.

Instantly, we froze. I held my fork still poised in midair in front of my face.

Mo's hearing was so finely tuned he could sense when a lightbulb was about to burn out or the breeze changing direction—sounds that were much too quiet for the rest of us to pick up on.

"What is it?" Grace whispered. She held tight to her bowl as she stood, creeping over to the single window in the room. It faced the road, but a thick brown curtain lay draped across it, preventing anyone from seeing inside.

Click.

"I heard it that time," Leo's voice was barely audible. "Do you think we were followed? Nikki, did you watch your back on the way here?"

I looked longingly at the bowl of noodles in my hand. Was it too much to ask for *ten minutes* of quiet to sit and enjoy a meal without running for my life?!

"Of course," I hissed. Setting the bowl down beside me, I held my breath.

The sound returned. *Click.*

Click click.

Someone was definitely at the front door, trying to quietly open it. Pretty soon, they'd be kicking it down.

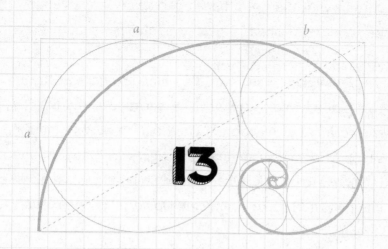

13

I snatched Pickles from the floor so she wouldn't investigate the window and shift the curtains. Nobody could know we were here.

But it looked like we were too late. *Had* I been followed? Was I not only the late one but also the sloppy escapee who'd let herself be tailed? The cold sweat of shame crept over my exhausted body.

"Hold still . . ." Grace let out a long, slow exhale. Her arms hung at her sides and her fingertips wiggled slightly. The heel of her right foot shifted ever so slightly, sending her weight to her toe.

I'd seen it a hundred times before.

She was preparing to run.

Leaning back against the wall, she moved the

curtain with the tip of her finger, nearly imperceptibly. Recognition flashed in her eyes, and her mouth grew tight.

"Everyone . . ." she said. She shifted on her toes again. Her gaze moved to the array of backpacks and laptops spread around the room. "There's a crawlspace on the second floor. It's a hidden passage that loops around the house to outside. Once you get to the street, break off into pairs and make a run for it. Do *not* all go in the same direction."

"Where do we meet?" Mary's voice was strained and sharp. Beside her, Charlie rolled her shoulders and stretched her neck from side to side.

Grace's eyebrows knit together as she ran through the layout of the city in her head. "The pizza place by Tower Bridge. Get the Circle line there. Spread out on the cars. Bring whatever you can carry. Go!"

At Grace's instruction, all heck broke loose.

We dove toward our collection of safe-house backpacks, grabbing whatever we could and bounding our way up the stairs. We moved so quickly that I barely had time to wrangle Pickles and nearly tripped over Bert's long legs on the way.

"Stop right where you are!" A loud voice boomed below us, yards away from the staircase. Then,

BANG!—something erupted in the sitting room where we'd been moments earlier. The clatter of broken porcelain rang out through the stairwell; whoever had busted into our house had crashed into the messy pile of dishes we'd left on the floor.

"Not good!" I yelped. *"Not good!"*

We clamored up the stairs in a raucous, shifting heap and bolted for the crawlspace exit. Panting hard, Grace stood by the small hole in the wall and ushered us through it. Charlie, Mary, Bert, Mo, Leo . . . everyone ducked into the dark crawlspace, leaving behind nothing but the trailing sound of footsteps on the secret passage's cold cement steps as they raced off.

"Grace!" I motioned for her to go ahead of me. "Get *out* of here!"

She shook her head and waved me forward, then gripped me by the strap of my backpack and hauled me closer. "You first! Go! I'll follow behind!"

"Don't move a muscle!" I recognized the voice. The pounding of heavy shoes on the floor told me that Agent Donnelly was right behind us, and he wouldn't take kindly to me slipping out on him again.

So much for a safe house.

Cursing my mistake, I lunged forward into the darkness. The others had gotten a small head start. They could still get away. But would Grace? *Why hadn't I covered my tracks better?!*

There was no time to think of that now. I focused instead on the panicked, labored sound of my breathing and the slapping of my feet against the concrete as I ran down the passage as fast as I could. Pickles clung to my shoulder for dear life.

Grace's footsteps echoed right behind me, and within seconds she shot past me, quick as a bullet. I'd forgotten that Grace was part cheetah. We were going to make it!

We burst onto the street, our safe little home far behind us. I already missed the food and computers and everything else we needed to survive.

Keeping pace with Grace out of pure panic, we bounded into the closest tube station, leaped onto the first train that came, and kept moving, hastily weaving around the passengers until we found a quiet spot to catch our breaths.

"Tesla!" Grace gasped as she doubled over from exertion and pointed to the underground map on the wall. "Eight stops," she panted. "Then we get off this train."

I nodded once, and as we pulled into the next station, I prepared myself for the inevitable face of Agent

Donnelly waiting on the platform. The doors to the car beeped in warning, then opened widely for the next wave of passengers.

But he wasn't there.

A very tense half hour later, the seven of us met outside the agreed-upon pizza shop. Scanning every one of my friends from head to toe, my shoulders relaxed slightly. We'd successfully evaded Agent Donnelly! For once, I couldn't believe our luck. Outsmarting a skilled agent was one thing. But doing it *twice* was practically a miracle.

So why weren't they happier?

Leo looked the worst, with weary eyes and a strained, resigned frown on his face. I couldn't take any more bad news today, but had to ask.

"What is it?" I grabbed his hand instinctively. "Tell us so we can fix it, Leo."

He solemnly held up his phone, displaying the tiny white screen for us to read. The presidential logo sat proudly at the top. Grace took the phone and flicked over the page with her thumb.

"The president has shut us down," she said, shaking her head in disgust.

Charlie wiped her forehead with her sleeve. "What do you mean *us*?"

Grace tossed the phone back to Leo, then let her hands drop angrily at her sides. "I mean *us*—all of us. Martha's been detained at MI6 and will be handed over to the American government. All operatives investigating Victor are still compromised, and the president has a warrant out for our arrests because of what happened at the Tower of London. *All* of us. We're not safe here. And now we're not safe at home."

It was like running into a brick wall. One minute I was moving fast, with the scenery whipping by around me.

And the next?

Smash.

Mary asked the question going through my mind, even though I was afraid I already knew the answer. "What about Genius Academy?"

Grace leveled her dark eyes on Mary. Her expression confirmed my biggest fear. "What *about* it?" She clicked her tongue in annoyance. "We're wanted for stealing one of the world's most priceless diamonds, and the head of the Academy has been arrested on conspiracy."

"That means . . . ?" I braced for the worst.

Grace's jaw clenched and she stared forward with stony eyes. "It means there *is* no Genius Academy."

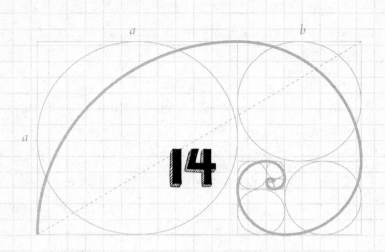

14

"This is madness!"

Charlie was in the middle of a world-class freak-out, and since we were all stuck in the back of a pizza place on a crowded city street, we couldn't exactly get away from her. I leaned against the window and shifted my backpack on my lap.

"They're shutting us down because they think we nicked some posh diamond?!" She flung her hands into the air, sending her fork clanging from the table.

Mary leaned over to retrieve it, wiping it on the hem of her shirt before placing it back beside Charlie.

Here's a quick summary of what happened when we learned that Genius Academy had indeed been shut down and that we were all officially homeless in a foreign country. No safe house. No Martha. Not even a bowl of macaroni and cheese to our name.

1. Bert squealed and nearly fainted.
2. Mary cried.
3. Grace consoled Mary.
4. Leo sighed very loudly.
5. Mo grunted in annoyance.
6. I sunk down to my knees in a bout of dizzy sadness.
7. And Charlie? Well, Charlie absolutely lost her marbles.

Which, as you can probably guess by the noise, she was still in the process of doing.

"We have private jets at our disposal. People with private jets don't need to steal jewels. What are we going to do?! Hiding in some pizza shop isn't going to help anything!"

Grace set her jaw, but so far hadn't reacted to Charlie's outburst. "I told you, Charlie," she repeated calmly. "With those agents after us, our best chance is to lie low. You know how many surveillance cameras pepper the streets of London? We'd be caught within hours. This is our chance to regroup without eyes on us. We're not leaving this restaurant until we have a plan. A *real* one."

Charlie rolled her eyes and began pacing around our table. "But what can we possibly do?! We need the Academy! We can't even go back to the States—they have all our documents! The Academy's our home, and they've shut it down all because of an ancient"—she kicked the air—"ridiculous"—*another kick*—"rock!"

Bert lifted his finger and grimaced, dodging out of the way of one of Charlie's air kicks. "Technically, they probably shut us down for organizing a global operation to steal said diamond while simultaneously endangering the lives of thousands of people at what is probably the most famous historical landmark in the world. Just wanted to clarify that."

Charlie scoffed. "But it was a setup! Anyone with two brain cells could see it!" Her face paled as she continued to put together the problem. "And *Martha*?!" She whirled around and pointed her finger at Grace. "How could they think Martha is some rogue thief or terrorist? She's got more decency and integrity in her pinkie toe than every one of those daft MI6 agents combined!"

Grace stood up and got between Charlie and the rest of us to shield us from those long runner's legs of hers.

"Okay," Grace said, lifting her hands in the air. She started pacing around our table. "We've got to get it together here. We *aren't* homeless."

Bert raised an eyebrow. "Well, the Academy is off-limits for the time being, along with most of our belongings, so I'd say we are."

Grace's brow furrowed. *"No."* She shook her fist. "Our home isn't the *building* we live in! That's just where we keep our stuff."

I exchanged glances with Leo, who seemed equally intrigued by Grace's change in demeanor. It wasn't like her to get up and give some big speech. Clearly things weren't working in our favor if she was bringing out the pep talk already.

"*We* are home." Grace spread her arms wide, motioning to all of us. "Don't you get it? *We* are Genius Academy. Each one of us. We all bring something unique to our team, and together, it's a lot more than the sum of its parts."

Charlie opened her mouth, then closed it again. A timid smile grew on her face. Her cheeks, which had been red with frustration moments ago, began to pale to their usual color.

"Grace is right," Mary said, sitting up straighter. "We don't need Genius Academy. We are Genius Academy." She lifted her chin at Grace and gave her the tiniest nod.

Solidarity.

"Err, that's all very lovely and poetic, you two," Bert muttered. "But somewhere out there, a virus is set to destroy humanity, and the last time I checked, we needed to stop it, right? So as squishy and heartfelt as this all sounds, what do we actually *do* here? Hugs won't save the world."

I bit my lip. As much as I liked Grace's speech, I found myself agreeing with Bert. The seven of us might be the heart of Genius Academy, but that didn't help us get the resources we needed to complete any missions. Money, passports, tickets, state-of-the-art computer systems—they were all vital to our success. You can't fight evil with love and heart. Sometimes, you need actual weapons to go with them.

Grace put her hands on her hips and turned to Bert. "Let's start with what we know. What were you going to tell us before we were so rudely interrupted by our agent friend at the safe house?"

Bert pulled the only laptop we'd managed to hang on to from his backpack. "Oh, is Charlie done freaking out now?" He gave her a half-hearted grin. "Because Leo and I uncovered something really important about Victor's virus."

On cue, Leo cracked his knuckles and took the laptop from Bert's hands. Fingertips flying over the keys, he bit his lower lip the way he always did when he was concentrating hard. If I wasn't worried about being stuck in England for the rest of my life without a passport, I'd have thought he looked adorable.

Okay, he *did* look adorable.

"There's an antidote," Leo said plainly.

Grace's jaw dropped. "There is?!" She pumped her fist in the air, beaming. "Yes! This changes everything!"

"Not so fast," Bert said. He cleared his throat. "We also discovered that Victor is planning on selling it."

Mary frowned. "When?"

"Four days from now," Leo replied. "He plans to meet his buyer at St Bartholomew's Hospital at two p.m."

Charlie tapped her chin with her forefinger, already excited to be scheming. "So it's simple. We need to infiltrate that meeting and steal the antidote. It's the only way to clear our names."

"Uh . . . *and* save the world from a horrific virus, too," Mo added, glancing warily at Charlie.

She waved her hand dismissively. "Right, that too. Details."

Mo continued. "Couldn't we just steal the virus itself and call it a day?"

Leo frowned. "That would be ideal, but . . ."

"We have no idea where the serum is," Grace said, yawning.

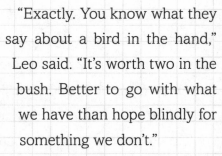

"Exactly. You know what they say about a bird in the hand," Leo said. "It's worth two in the bush. Better to go with what we have than hope blindly for something we don't."

"A bird in the hand will poop on you." Charlie plunked down beside Bert and squinted at the laptop screen. "But you're right. If we have a shot at capturing the antidote, we need to do it. That way, if the worst happens and Victor unleashes the virus, we can make sure everyone gets the antidote."

"We need disguises," Mary said. "We've been spotted way too many times by MI6, and now that we've escaped for a second time, they'll be on the lookout for us everywhere."

Mo drummed his fingers on his knee. "We can't exactly stack two of us on top of each other and put on a trench coat, you know. What other options are there?"

"Forget the disguises." Bert shook his head with a huff. "We need to figure out *when* to strike. Do we go in early and steal the antidote before Victor meets with whoever's buying it? Or do we let the exchange happen and *then* steal it?"

"We're going to need access to the elevators and security cameras," Leo pointed out. He looked down glumly at his backpack. "I don't have a lot of equipment, but I can make something work. Maybe."

"You don't sound very confident," I said, resting a hand on his shoulder.

He shrugged. "I'm trying to be realistic," he said. "Heists, break-ins, disguises . . . this is why the Academy was so great. Without those resources . . ."

Charlie's mouth twisted into a tight grimace. "Without any help from the Academy," she continued for him, "it's going to be next to impossible to pull this off. Isn't it?"

I scratched Pickles behind the ear and cleaned some of the congealed macaroni and cheese from her furry mouth with my napkin.

"What do you think, huh?" I asked her, half joking. She couldn't answer, of course, but that didn't stop me from imagining what she would say. Since joining the Academy, we'd seen a lot of impossible things. Kids who could save the world. Rings that could change anyone into any form they wanted. I'd even found that *friendship* was no longer hopeless for me, something that I'd never have believed a year ago. In fact, I was beginning to think people like us were making the impossible possible every day. What was stopping us from doing it again?

"When I was in custody, Martha told me that the most difficult problems require elementary solutions," I said. "We just have to go back to basics. I mean, we've done it before, right? Like, with—"

"Wait," Mary interrupted. "Did Martha actually use the word *elementary* in your conversation?"

I thought back to the tiny room with the handcuffs. "Um, yeah?" I blinked. "When she visited me in my interrogation room."

A small, nervous smile crossed Mary's face. "Of course!" she whispered.

"What do you know that we don't, Mary?" Bert asked. He looked to Leo and Charlie, who simply shrugged. They were as confused as he was.

"*Elementary,*" Mary said. She was talking to herself now, with an air of uncertainty and hesitation. "It's our only option. We're in the United Kingdom after all; it's not that far. Maybe we could . . ." She trailed off, then turned to face us. "I know what Martha was trying to tell us," she said. "I know where we need to go."

"And where's that?" Grace asked.

"Scotland." Mary pulled a stack of papers from her backpack, unfolded one of them, and spread it across the table.

"What's in Scotland besides the Loch Ness monster?" I asked.

She crossed her arms over her chest. "Tech. Weapons. Surveillance. And most importantly, a friend."

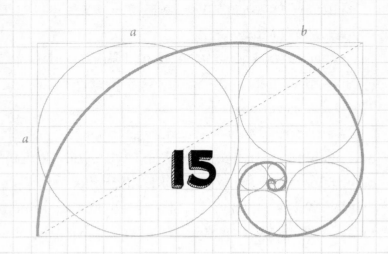

15

I craned my neck up at the cracked and towering stone turrets above our heads, marveling at the way the highest peaks poked through the Scottish fog.

None of us knew who Mary's mysterious *friend* was, and she wasn't giving anything away, but they were the best option we had, so we'd hopped on a train and headed to Edinburgh, Scotland's capital city. It had taken hours, but as the distance between us and Agent Donnelly had grown wider, I began breathing a little easier.

Ever since I'd first set eyes on the Genius Academy mansion, with its zillion rooms, pristine laboratories, and year-round ice cream truck, I thought I'd seen the best living space the world had to offer.

But you know what? It turns out a mansion *wasn't* the

coolest place to live. That honor went to the huge, turreted fortress we now stood in front of. Every creepy, mossy inch of it.

"A castle?" I choked out a laugh. "Your friend lives in a *castle?*" I reached forward to place my hand on the cool stone, enchanted by the lush tendrils of green ferns that seemed to reach up from the ground to hug the ancient stone foundation. "Why do we have a mansion, when we could have a castle?"

"We *don't* have a mansion anymore, remember?" Bert said bitterly. He was still in a bad mood because Grace had cut lunch short. His stomach rumbled. "Do you think this friend of yours knows how to make a grilled cheese sandwich, Mary?"

Mary pursed her lips, ignoring him. Ever since boarding the train to the city, she'd become increasingly hard to read. She was nervous, quieter than usual, and even a bit . . . distracted. She kept staring off into the distance and spacing out during conversations.

"All right, everyone." She forced a tight smile. "When we get inside, try not to judge my friend. He's a little . . . *different.*"

"You're saying this to six geniuses who are currently wanted for grand larceny by the British government. Different is kind of our thing," Leo pointed out.

"Three cheers for Team Different," Charlie mused, popping a piece of gum into her mouth and chomping loudly.

"But still!" Mary hissed. She smoothed her hair, then applied a slick coat of lip gloss from a tube in her pocket.

I glanced at Charlie. This friend of Mary's was getting more interesting by the second, and we hadn't even met him yet.

"Hey, Mary . . ." I ventured. "How exactly do you know this guy?"

"We don't have time for the long story," she said softly. "Is everyone ready?"

She knocked on the castle door, and within seconds, a quiet shuffling sounded behind the massive door. I was expecting someone big and hulking to answer, fitting in with the size of the enormous castle.

But instead, a tiny woman in a muted purple dress appeared at the door. The deep lines on her face starkly contrasted the perfectly pressed white apron across her waist, and the tiniest pair of reading glasses that I'd ever seen was perched on the top of her head, tucked into a nest of graying hair.

"Mary?" The woman's mouth dropped open. "Oh, Mary, my dear! It has been an *age*!" I sidestepped to make room for her as she rushed forward to wrap Mary in her arms.

"Mrs. Hudson!" she exclaimed. She returned the woman's hug, rocking from side to side for a few moments. "I'm so sorry for dropping in on you unannounced. I know you hate that." She gave her an apologetic bow.

Mrs. Hudson straightened out her apron and finally moved her gaze to take in the rest of us. What must she have thought of the seven of us? Showing up with dirty backpacks; messy, running-from-the-authorities hair; and crazed, desperate looks in our eyes.

"Nonsense," Mrs. Hudson said. "You know you're always welcome here, Mary. That includes any friends of yours, as well. Come in, come in! Get out of those wet shoes. Edinburgh is dreadfully damp this time of year. Dreadfully damp *any* time of year, matter of fact. Best to warm up by the fire."

"Thank you," Mary said gratefully. We stepped inside the castle and immediately were met with a fire crackling to our left in an enormous fireplace and a sweeping wave of stairs dominating the center of the hall. It was like stepping back in time.

"Everyone"—Mary gestured to the old woman—"this is Mrs. Hudson. She's caretaker of this place. She's also a pretty great cook."

Bert perked up, twisting around in search of the kitchen. "You don't say?"

Mrs. Hudson bent a few degrees into the tiniest curtsy. "Pleased to meet you all."

Mary grinned, but the nervous glint didn't disappear from her face. That told me that Mrs. Hudson, despite her hospitality, wasn't the only one we'd be meeting today.

"And, Mrs. Hudson," Mary said, "these are my friends. From Genius Academy."

I shifted back on my heels, surprised that she would share information about Genius Academy like that. Wasn't it supposed to be a government secret? But Mrs. Hudson didn't flinch. How did this teensy castle caretaker know about us already?

"Leo, Grace, Charlie," Mary continued, "Mo, Bert, and that's Nikki." She pointed to us all, and we each nodded when introduced. "We need your help."

Mrs. Hudson plucked the tiny glasses from her head and squinted through them, frowning dolefully through the dirty lenses. "You need *my* help?" she asked as she used the hem of her skirt to wipe the glass. "Or . . ."

Mary's voice rose an octave. "*His* help," she admitted. "We need his help."

Mrs. Hudson let out a slow whoosh of a sigh. "I'd be happy to help you all, Mary." She spoke slowly, and I didn't miss the tone of sympathy in her words. A sinking feeling began to grow in my stomach. Sympathy was never promising. "But you know he's very particular about his time. And things have never quite been the same since . . . well, you know."

"I do," Mary said. "But we don't have any other choice. The Academy's been shut down. If he doesn't help us . . ." She trailed off. "I don't want to think about what could happen. It could be the end of everything."

We all stood still as statues as Mrs. Hudson scrutinized us, ending with Mary. "All right," she said. "If anyone could convince him, it's you." She gave Mary a wink. "Now come along. He's upstairs."

"What the heck does that mean?" Charlie whispered to me. "She makes it sound like Mary and this guy were, like . . . *you know* . . ."

"No idea," I admitted. A small trickle of annoyance dripped through me. Mary knew all *my* secrets; shouldn't I know all hers?

We followed Mrs. Hudson and Mary like a flock of ducks chasing their mother, our damp socks squishing as we waddled up the grand staircase.

It took us about seven minutes of navigating stone hallways lined with gold-framed portraits of generations of uptight British geriatrics to finally reach the door that Mrs. Hudson was looking for.

"Hello?" she called out. She knocked once gently on the door and cracked it open, revealing a dark room filled wall-to-wall with bookshelves. Against a large window sat a mahogany desk, and instead of facing the door, its accompanying chair was turned away from us, looking upon the gray outside world. The brown elbow of a shirt-sleeve peeked out on one side.

"Mrs. Hudson!" The elbow shifted, hiding its owner from view. "You know I've asked not to be bothered while I'm writing! I've only just sat down for the day!" The voice didn't sound much older than the rest of us.

Bert leaned down to mutter in my ear. "He's a writer, like Mary!"

I held my breath. Something about the stillness of the room amplified every creak of the floor and shuffle in that gigantic, overstuffed leather chair in front of us. And every shaky breath from Mary as she stepped forward.

"It's not Mrs. Hudson," she said as the dark silhouette of an arm reached forward, a quill pen in hand. The arm froze instantly in midair at the sound of Mary's voice.

I made a face at Charlie. *Who writes with a quill pen these days?*

The tension in the air was giving me a headache, but I was too spooked by the eerie Victorian room to speak out of turn. I wouldn't have been surprised if ghosts were listening in on us.

"Mary Wollstonecraft Shelley." The boy drew out her name, like he was inspecting every syllable. The chair creaked again, and he set the feather quill down on the surface of his immaculate desk. He was still facing away from us, shrouded by the tall back of his ornate chair.

"Yes," Mary answered. Bert cleared his throat awkwardly.

"You're not alone. There are five others . . ." The boy sniffed loudly, then corrected himself. "No, six."

I turned to Leo, more than a little perturbed. Were there surveillance cameras all over the castle? Could he somehow *smell* us? Spiders of suspicion began to crisscross my neck.

Mary set her hand on her hip and dropped her backpack at her feet, startling all of us. "Yep, congratulations, you're right. As always," she said. Her timid attitude was gone, replaced by something I'd never really seen before: an *edgy* Mary. Pushy and almost sarcastic. "So are you going to help us or what?" she asked.

"Uh, Mary?" Charlie ventured, stepping forward. "Maybe we should ask a little bit . . . *nicer*? Nicer than that, anyway. And explain what's going on?"

"Oh, he already knows. Don't you, Artie?"

A floorboard groaned as the chair shifted back, its wooden legs protesting loudly. The boy sidestepped his desk and turned to face us.

Finally, I was able to get a good look at him . . . and honestly? I hate to say it, but he was pretty darn *cute*.

Not like, *Leo* cute, maybe. But the kid had tousled, thick black hair, sharp yet kind eyes, and dark skin. He wore black pants and a brown sweater, and his hands were stained with patches of ink.

But cute or not, I still hadn't sorted out how exactly Mary was expecting this kid to help us steal the antidote to Victor's virus. Was he going to help us *write* the bad guy to death or something? Maybe throw a quill pen at him?

"Let me guess," he said, tilting his head in amusement, his cool gaze passing over each of us. "Genius Academy has been disavowed and shut down completely. Martha has been arrested, and you seven have been framed for not only stealing the Crown Jewels but also for an explosion at the Tower of London. You each escaped arrest not long ago, and you've since lost your safe house because someone . . ." He scanned the group, landing squarely on me, and pointed. "*You*. You're the one. Because *this one* with the ferret was followed by British intelligence. And now you've had no choice but to head north to Edinburgh to the one person you know who can help you prevent the destruction of mankind. What is it you're trying to stop?" He chewed his lip. "Something huge. Something . . . biological."

In my periphery, Leo's eyebrows lifted in surprise. He was impressed.

I was impressed, too, if we're being honest. How on earth did he know all that?

"A deadly virus," Mary said. A small grin played at her lips, but she was trying to hide it with attitude.

"*Ah*, so close." The boy shook his head in mock frustration. "Nearly had that one."

The two stared at her each for a beat.

"*Awkward . . .*" Bert said, covering his mouth with his hand as he half coughed the word.

Mary jerked back to reality, blinking wildly. "Right," she said. "Everyone, this is Artie. Artie, this is—"

"*Wait.*" The boy interrupted her. "How many times do I have to tell you, Wollstonecraft? It's not Artie . . ." He gave her a devilish grin. "It's *Arthur.*"

He turned to our leader, instinctively knowing who was in charge. "Grace, I presume. I'm Arthur Conan Doyle. Detective. Author. Mary's ex-boyfriend. At your service."

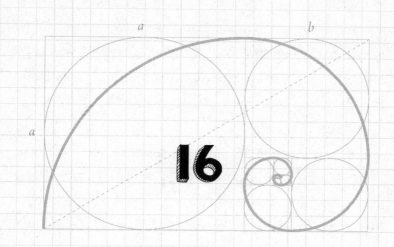

16

"What?!" I exclaimed. How could Mary have kept a secret this big?!

Arthur clicked his tongue, clearly enjoying my reaction. "Oh, has she not told you about me?" He gave Mary a pouty look, clutching his chest dramatically. "That hurts, Wollstonecraft."

Mary rolled her eyes. "Don't start, Artie," she said. "I wouldn't be here unless it was our last option. I *know* you don't like random people dropping in on you."

He crossed his arms. "You're not random people."

Mary's attitude softened. "So you'll help us? We've got a theft to organize and could use some of your tech."

"I typically spend my time pursuing thieves and

criminals, Mary. To *prevent* robberies. I'm currently tracking someone who's been hopping all over the United
Kingdom stealing millions of dollars from high-security
organizations." He crossed his arms over his chest haughtily. "Now you want me to *become* a criminal? A thief like
all the rest of them?"

Mary mirrored his posture, tapping her toe impa-
tiently. "Like you haven't been a criminal before," she
said. "We both know you'll never be like anyone else.
Please, you're our only hope. Almost all our belongings
were at a Genius Academy safe house. We don't even
have a place to sleep."

He glanced over at me. "Because this one got followed to your safe house, right?"

"*This one* has a name, you know," I huffed, glowering
at him. Pickles chattered angrily in my defense.

He bowed slightly. "Of course you do. My apologies.
I'm not used to having company, as Mary has pointed
out. You are, of course, Nikola Tesla. Inventor, newest
recruit at the Academy, and ... ferret owner." He
extended his hand.

I shook it, once again feeling those creepy edges of
suspicion crawl over me. "How do you know that? And
more importantly, how do you know about the Crown
Jewels? And Martha's arrest?"

"How do people know *anything*, really?" he asked. "It's all deduction. Elementary, my dear Nikola."

A chill ran up my spine at his words.

"Artie..." Mary's voice was a low warning. "Behave. These are my friends."

He lifted his hands and raised his thick eyebrows in mock innocence. "What? What did I do? Nikki asked a question! I'm allowed to answer questions, aren't I?"

"Ugh," Mary said. "I *knew* this would happen! You can't help it, can you? Could you please go five whole minutes without... without... being *yourself*!" she sputtered, squeezing her hands into fists. "Artie's kind of like me. But instead of reading people's emotions, he's more of a..." She trailed off, searching for the right word.

"Genius?" Artie offered.

"Um, *no*! I was going to say 'computer.' He puts a lot of things together at once. Though the *result* can be more than annoying." Mary glared at him.

"So you know what's happened because you've *deduced* it?" Charlie asked. Her lip curled in skepticism.

Arthur bit his lip and looked to Mary, as though he was asking permission.

"Go ahead." She waved her hands dismissively. "Show them."

To my great terror, he turned to stare at me. "Every-one wears their guilt in different ways," he said.

I didn't know where he was going with this, but I was pretty sure it wouldn't be fun for me.

"Uh-huh . . ." I said, shrinking away from his stare.

He reached up, nearly touching my face. "Nikki here wears her guilt on her left nostril. You see how it flares a

traitorous
nostril
flaring with
guilt

little when I mention your safe house being discovered? All I had to do was pay attention. Everyone has a tell."

I forced my chin higher. "My *nostril* isn't doing any-thing!" I said haughtily.

"Whoa, it is!" Bert said. "Look at that! Flaring up like a balloon!" He leaned in closer to inspect my face. I swat-ted him away with one hand.

"And you . . ." Artie turned to Bert, who sidestepped away, as though physically moving would protect him from Artie's observations.

"What *about* me?" Bert challenged. He leaned closer to Charlie, like she might protect him, too.

"Albert Einstein," Artie said. "No, wait . . ." He scrutinized him some more. His face took on that faraway stare-at-the-wall quality he'd had earlier. "Not Albert. You don't like that, do you? It's *Bert*. Albert reminds you of an old man."

Bert blinked at him, suddenly looking about two inches tall, compared to his usual giraffe-esque stature.

"You don't know that," Bert said. "I go by Albert sometimes."

Mary snorted in response. "You're not going to fool him, Bert."

Artie continued. "You, *Bert*, have one sister. It makes you extra empathetic to the girls in your life, though you lack the skills to demonstrate it. You prefer to be behind a laptop screen or buried beneath stacks of research." He paused and lifted his chin playfully. "Does she know, Bert?"

Bert swallowed. "Does . . . does who know what?" he squeaked. In a matter of seconds, his cheeks went from beet red to nearly white.

Artie exhaled loudly, amused at his own brilliance. "Is

that enough?" he asked casually, grinning at Mary. "Or can we crack on?"

"No way," Charlie shouted. "Now do me!" She clambered by Bert to get closer to Artie.

"I'm not a circus act!" Artie said, backing away from her.

"Pleaaase?" she asked, clutching her hands like a prayer.

"Fine, fine . . ." he said. "You're an easy mark, Charlotte Darwin. Animal hair all over your shirt. The Academy's resident biologist. There are remnants of dirt under the fingernails of your hand, but the dirt from the first three fingernails differs from the dirt on your ring and pinkie finger, so you've also recently been doing some controlled experiments on soil . . . likely to ascertain the most suitable environment for the collection of snails you've been gathering from Genius Academy grounds in the past two months."

Charlie pinched her mouth into a tight line, then a devious expression crossed over her face. "Sure, all that's the easy stuff," she teased. "What's my favorite color?"

Every head in the room swiveled back to Artie, as though we were watching a very nerdy tennis match.

Artie didn't miss a beat. "This one thinks it's blue," he said, pointing to Bert. "But it is one hundred percent, most definitely green."

"Ha!" Bert yelped, pointing at him. "You're wrong! Her favorite *is* blue! I know this because we all chipped in and got her a bright blue bike for her birthday!"

"Oh, dear," Artie said, looking to Charlie. "Should you tell them, or should I?"

Charlie bowed her head sheepishly. "I really *love* the bike, guys!" she said. "But . . ."

"Oh, you've got to be kidding me!" Bert wailed, throwing his arms up. "I asked you! I asked you specifically! I said, *'Hey, Charlie, what's your favorite color?'* And you said, *'BLUE!'*" He shoved his glasses back up onto his nose and glared at her.

"I know!" Charlie cried. "I'm sorry! I was in the middle of my soil samples when you asked, and you were standing so close to my snails, I would have said anything to get you out of there! I thought you were going to crush them!" She couldn't hide her laughter. "I didn't realize till you'd left what you were even asking!"

"I think we've heard enough," Grace said with a weary sigh. "We need to focus on stealing the antidote."

"And what's your plan?" Artie asked.

"We know our suspect is selling it in three days' time. They're meeting at St Bart's Hospital, back in London. We're going to let the swap happen, and when the buyer

tries to leave, we'll stop the elevators, administer a mild sedative, and pocket the antidote while he's passed out. No violence. No witnesses."

Artie's lower lip puckered out. "Well, that sounds boring."

"*Artie* . . ." Mary warned again.

"Fine, fine." He lifted his hands in apology. "It's a great plan. It can work."

"Thanks," Grace said. "You're not the only smart one in the room." She sounded serious, but the playful twinkle in her eyes gave her away. Already, she respected Arthur. "So you're in? You'll help us?"

"I will," Arthur said. "But we should get started right away. We've only got three days to get this right."

"Agreed," Leo said. "Let's start with the elevator. Do you have a computer I could borrow?"

Arthur breezed past us out the door, turning over his shoulder to answer. "I rather think we should start with something else, Leo. All of you, follow me!"

"Where are we going?" Charlie asked as we made our way down the ancient hallway. It was the question all of us were thinking.

Arthur marched us down a long, twisted staircase. "To my lab. It's time for a little target practice."

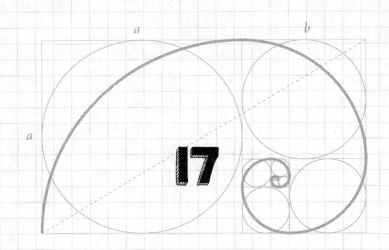

"I know I said I was on board with this mission, but nobody said anything about dangling from the ceiling of a castle wearing ten bathrobes like a sloppy disco ball!" Bert's voice echoed from above my head.

I couldn't blame him. Suspended from the ballroom's high ceiling with a set of raggedy ropes tied around his middle like a harness, Bert was red-faced, annoyed, and not afraid to show it.

It was officially time for Operation Poison Dart Frog.

Operation Poison Dart Frog had three phases. Mo, Charlie, and Leo were in charge of Phase 1. They were using some of Artie's tech to figure out a way to control the elevators so we could stop them between floors remotely.

Arthur and I were responsible for Phase 2, which involved my specialty: invention! We had to design a robot that could shoot a tranquilizer dart from a distance so we could successfully sedate the buyer.

Then Mary, Charlie, and Grace would nab the antidote when the buyer was knocked out and get us out of there without being caught. That was Phase 3.

Easy enough, right? At least, it would have been if we could get the stupid robot to work.

"Quit complaining," I yelled back. "The bathrobes are for your protection! You want to get shot at without them?" Fiddling with the knobs of Artie's invention, I swiveled a small metal tube to tighten my aim on Bert. "Incoming!"

Another dart shot from the tube, zinging through the air and narrowly missing Bert's knee.

"Ha!" he cried. "Missed me!" Bert yanked on his ropes with one arm and kicked the air in triumph.

"I'll get you next time, Einstein." I glared at him, taking a sip from the iced tea that Mrs. Hudson had brought us for hydration during our little experiment.

Once Arthur and I had repurposed one of his old robots to shoot tranquilizer darts, I'd sweet-talked a laptop out of Leo and connected the robot wirelessly to a primitive targeting system, which operated based on simple directions and commands using a coordinate system.

I have to admit, despite missing my own academy lab space, there was something epic about working in a castle.

When we'd left his study, I'd been surprised to find out that Arthur, besides being extremely gifted with the powers of deduction, was also something of an inventor himself. He'd led us to his spacious ballroom-turned-laboratory, with treasures and trinkets lining every shelf. My fingers skimmed over rusted copper flying contraptions, water-stained beakers and chipped vases of every size, metal bicycles, ornate prosthetic limbs, and handheld weapons with rivets dotting their sides. In the corner, what looked to be a Victorian motorcycle with dusty headlamps stared at us like the eyes of a steampunk dragonfly.

It was spectacular.

The only catch? Everything in his lab was *ancient*.

"Have you ever thought about adding in some more . . . *recent* materials to your lab, Arthur? We've come a long way since the 1800s," I said, wiping my oil-stained fingers on the front of my pants.

He shrugged. "Mary used to tease me about it, but I've always enjoyed working with historical technology.

There's something fun about bringing something back to life."

I peered into the small viewfinder of our robot, aiming again at Bert's dangling legs.

"Round three!" I shouted. "Heads up!" I hit the small button on the robot and watched a fake dart fly toward Bert, missing his elbow.

"Argh!" I threw the screwdriver in my hands down to the ground. "Why can't I get this thing to aim properly?! Should we just point it manually rather than worry about the targeting system?"

Bert wagged his finger at me from above. "Maybe *you* should be up here, Tesla! Leave the mechanics to a real inventor!" He cackled loudly, swishing his feet around in a sarcastic jig.

"Oh, stuff it, Einstein." I glowered up at him. "I should program this thing to respond to your voice so you have to spend the rest of your life running from my little poison darts! Or fill some balloon grenades with glitter paint so you can look like the disco ball you're so afraid of becoming. Whatever wipes that smirk off your face."

"That's not a bad idea." Arthur grinned. "But you might want to tell your ferret to watch out."

"What?" I turned to find Pickles racing from beneath one of the tall benches, away from a clanging, metal disk that whirred along the floor after her. The name *Watson* was scrawled on its side in thick black letters.

"Is that...?" I pointed to the robot chasing her and laughed. It bonked against my feet, sending Pickles into a chattering tizzy on my shoulder.

"A remote vacuum cleaner, yes," Arthur said, grinning. "Named after an old friend. Don't tell Mrs. Hudson, but I feel bad that she's always having to clean up the castle. I designed several cleaning robots for each wing of the estate. She refuses to speak in front of them, though, so I have a feeling she thinks they're surveillance devices."

"Brilliant," I said. "I might have to borrow one for my lab."

"They do a terrible job of cleaning," he admitted. "But they're decent company in this big place."

I glanced up at him from where I knelt, loading our robot with another dart. The castle was cool, but the thought of spending my days here mostly alone made me weary.

"You know," I started. "We could use someone like you at Genius Academy." I kept my voice down so Bert couldn't hear me. It was pretty obvious that Arthur and Bert were destined to be two like charges, repelling each other at every turn.

Arthur's foot tapped beside me. "Martha tried to recruit me a couple of years ago," he said. "I turned her down."

I blinked at him. "Really? I had no idea!"

"Yep," he said. "Mary told me that I'd be stupid not to join the team, too." He grinned. "But I always felt more at home by myself. Plus, I could tell that being near me reminded Mary too much of . . ."

"Of what?" I asked.

"A time she'd rather forget," he said, bowing his head slightly. "We grew up together, and I think I remind her a lot of when her parents were still . . . around."

"Oh." The silence hung heavy between us as I tried to imagine what Mary was like before I knew her. She'd been through so much yet somehow had remained one of the kindest, cleverest people I knew.

Arthur broke the tension with a laugh. "And let's not forget that Bert would probably drop out of the Academy if I joined," he added.

"Bert's just Bert," I said, like that explained everything.

Arthur stared at me for a beat. "I'll think about it," he said.

"Good," I said, rolling one of the small darts in my palm. "Besides, we may be able to help you with your cases, too. Like that robbery stuff you were talking about. You could help us, and we could help you."

"Teamwork," he mused, quirking an eyebrow.

"Exactly!" I said.

"It would be nice to have another pair of eyes on this one case," he said. "Most robberies are pretty simple and straightforward, but something about this guy feels *different*. He's incredibly canny." He got that faraway expression on his face again, staring past me as I loaded the robot with another dart and sent it flying at Bert. This time it whizzed past his chest.

"How so?" The familiar prickle of curiosity niggled at me. If someone as smart as Arthur couldn't figure it out, it *had* to be a good case.

He hesitated for a moment, as if weighing whether he wanted to share more. Finally, though, he sifted through some of the dusty folders on his workspace desk and plopped one down in front of me. "See?" he said, running his finger down a column of numbers and names. "They always steal two million dollars at a time. But it's *who* they're targeting that has me worried."

I lifted the pages for a closer look. "PharmaTech ... BioSourceSolutions ... ChemStart ..." I frowned at Arthur. "They're stealing from science corporations?"

Arthur lit up. "Yes! Laboratories, pharmaceutical companies, even nonprofit organizations. They're targeting companies that make medicines and drugs, or do a lot of research into them. *Why?*"

I let out a sigh, shaking my head. "Sounds like they have a grudge against . . . science?" I offered. "Maybe it's not about the money. Maybe it's personal." I continued to page through the document, looking for something to connect them all.

"See, I thought of that," he said. "I even managed to track the thief down and get a visual, then used *that* to see if he was some disgruntled employee out for revenge."

"And?" I asked, hopeful.

"There was nothing," he said. "No connection whatsoever between Victor and the scientific community."

My heart skipped a beat, and the folder slipped from my hand, sending the papers scattering to the floor in a flurry.

"Hey!" Bert yelled from his ropes. "You okay down there, Nikki?"

"*Victor,*" I breathed. I turned to Arthur in shock, then immediately knelt down, frantically searching through the papers again. "His name is Victor?! Show me, Arthur—where is his picture? *Where is it?!*"

known bank robber

Arthur knelt beside me and swept the papers together in one big motion. "Here!" he said. "I got his picture from surveillance." He found the page he was looking for and placed it in my hands.

Familiar deep-set eyes stared back at me. It was the man with the dark hair who had smiled at me at the Tower of London.

"It's him!" I shouted, stabbing at the paper with my finger. "Holy guacamole, Arthur, it's *him!*"

"Who's him?" Leo's voice startled me. He and the others appeared in the ballroom doorway with concerned expressions. "And what's with all the shouting?"

I raced forward to the group and shoved the picture at Leo's face. "*Victor* is him!" I exclaimed. "Arthur had a picture from his own file on some robberies! We're tracking the same person!"

"What?!" Charlie yelped. "No way!" She snatched the photograph from me to examine it. "Robberies? Since when does this dude want money?"

"That's not all!" I stammered, too flabbergasted to speak clearly. "He's been targeting drug companies and research labs. He *only* steals from them."

Leo frowned. "So he's got a grudge, then? Is it personal?"

"That's what I said!" I said, my mind racing to put it all together. "But he's got no ties to anything related to science. Right, Arthur?"

"That's right," he said. His expression turned dark. "What are the odds that we're tracking the same person?"

Grace frowned. "My thoughts exactly." Her eyelids narrowed with suspicion.

"It's just a coincidence!" I said. "Sometimes we have to rely on luck when we're inventing stuff, right? That's all this is. We're *finally* getting a stroke of good luck. Arthur is after the same person we are!"

Arthur licked his lips. "I have to disagree, Nikki," he said.

"What?!" I said.

"I'm sorry, but I think we need to accept that there might be some *reason* we ended up tracking the same person, even though we live thousands of miles away from each other," he said. "There is no such thing as a coincidence."

I scoffed. "Oh, come on!" I said, waving my hands at the group. "Up until we showed up on your doorstep, what on earth connected our work? Tell me exactly *what* common thread there is between you pondering your cases up here alone in your castle and the missions Genius Academy undertakes!"

Arthur hesitated, his cheeks burning red. His mouth stayed clamped shut.

"See!" I slammed my hands down on my hips. "Nothing has changed—we still need to catch Victor and steal the antidote. But now we know a little more about him. This is *good* news!"

Grace clapped her hands together. "I agree," she said. "Maybe it's luck. Maybe it's not. But we have a job to do either way. I suggest we do it. Our tickets back to London are booked. We leave at dawn. We're getting that anti-dote if it's the last thing we do."

"Er...guys? What's everyone talking about?" Bert called from above. "Can someone let me down from here?"

I smiled at Mary, giving her the tiniest of winks. I knew how edgy she'd been on this trip so far, and a stroke of fortune had to make our task a little more man-ageable. With Arthur's help, we could catch this guy together!

But when I made eye contact with her, instead of her usual gentle and optimistic expression, her mouth was tight and creased with worry.

That's when it really hit me: Whatever we were facing in the days to come, Mary was afraid of it.

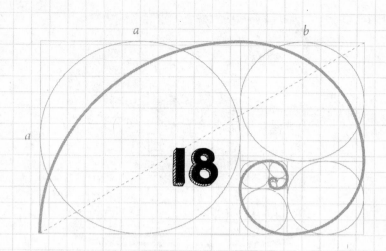

Exactly seventeen hours, forty-two minutes, and fifty-four seconds later, we were stationed in St Bartholomew's Hospital, waiting for the exact moment to strike.

How did I know the exact time? It turns out that when you're trying to fight the end of humanity as you know it, details matter. Also, Charlie had set her watch with a doomsday alarm and seemed to delight in ticking off each passing hour.

"One hour till Victor sells the antidote!" she warned us, tapping her watch to stop the high-pitched beeping. "It's getting real, everyone! Get your game faces on! Our names will be cleared by dinner!"

"I'm not sure that countdown is helpful, Chuck," Leo said, grimacing. He stretched his neck up and squirmed

London's oldest hospital

The history!

The monument!

The smell!!

away from Mo, whose elbow was smooshed directly in Leo's face. I swiped Charlie's swishing ponytail away from where Pickles sat on my shoulder and tried to summon as much patience as I could.

Oh, did I neglect to mention what we were up to? Sometimes, saving the world means you get to hang out in antiquated castles and invent robots that shoot sedatives at unsuspecting bad guys. But sometimes it means you have to cram eight people into one supply closet in a neglected corner of London's oldest hospital. And trust me, we'd all showered at Arthur's, but the cramped quarters and chemical smell from all the hospital cleaners was making it more than a little stinky in the room.

So far, St Bart's Hospital wasn't much to look at, but that's probably because I'd only been able to explore the ground-floor window we'd snuck inside during the night. And now the supply closet.

Gauze bandages, sterile alcohol wipes, and stacks of snow-white bleached sheets and towels towered over us on the metal shelves, along with IV poles, breathing tubes, surgical tape, disinfectants, and plastic IV bags.

There was something fitting about trying to steal a world-saving antidote in a hospital, but I could do without the bedpans brushing up against my earlobe.

"Focus, everyone!" Grace hissed. She braced herself against the wall, shoving the shelf beside her slightly to give her some more breathing room. "This should be quick and painless. Nikki, are you ready with Frog?"

Frog, of course, was what Arthur and I had named the robot that would fire the tranquilizer once Victor's associate was in the elevator.

"Yes," I said. I patted the leather bag strapped to my shoulder. "Once Leo has control of the elevator, I'll get Frog into the elevator shaft. Then all we need is for Charlie to do her job and make sure the buyer gets into the right elevator, alone."

"I'm on it!" Charlie saluted me, accidentally smacking Arthur in the temple with her outstretched elbow.

"Watch it!" he cried, rubbing his eye.

"Perfect," Grace said. "Nikki, take Mary with you in case she needs to provide a diversion while you're getting into position."

Mary lifted her chin fiercely. "I'll make sure she gets there."

Grace continued her instructions. "Arthur and Bert, you follow behind, but not too closely. You're on lookout. Thanks to Arthur, we've got a solid photo to use to identify Victor. Keep an eye out for the MI6 agents, too. Pretend you're here to see a relative and that you're waiting for visiting hours to begin. Take these." She passed them two comic books. "If anyone looks at you suspiciously, start reading."

"Got it," Bert said. "Arthur, this is called a comic book. Probably not nearly as fancy as the *classic literature* that you read in that castle, but you might find you enjoy it. This one's about a superhero who saves the world in his underwear."

"*Actually*, Bert," Arthur said, taking the pages from his hands, "I happen to love comic books. Research indicates that superior intellects benefit from the combination of both visual and textual information. Though I'm glad I get to wear more than just underwear on this mission," he added quickly.

"Oh boy," Charlie said. "Here they go again. The battle of wits, a never-ending saga by Bert and Arthur . . ."

"Hard to have a battle of wits when both are unarmed," Mary snapped.

"Oh! And there's Mary with the knockout!" Mo jeered, gleefully smacking his meaty fist into his open palm.

"Bert!" Grace scolded. "I've warned you once already! We need *everyone* to be at the top of their game today! No petty arguments. Both of you should know better! We're trying to stop people from getting sick and *dying*, remember?!"

"Yes, Grace," both Arthur and Bert intoned solemnly.

"Good!" Grace said, giving a stiff nod. She affixed one of my GeckoDots to her earlobe and gave it a tap so we would all be connected.

"Now everyone get going. Keep us updated on where you are. Leo, Mo, and I will stay here and get the elevator under control. When you've got our signal, you three get Nikki into position with Frog." She pointed at Bert, Arthur, and Mary.

"Do we go on three?" Arthur asked.

I blinked at him. "What do you mean?"

"You know," he said, "like everyone puts their hands in and we do a little *one, two, three, go team* or something? Isn't that what you do when you're about to tackle a big mission?"

Charlie grunted and wedged herself closer to the door of the closet, edging it open. A slice of light from the hospital hallway cut through the room, splitting us in half. "We're not that kind of team," she said.

Mary gave him a sympathetic smile. "We're more of a 'charge forward and hope for the best when everything goes wrong' kind of team."

"Hope? Is that the best strategy at a time like this?" Arthur's eyebrows lifted.

"Hey, we're still here, aren't we?" Bert clapped him on the back. "Let's go, *buddy*. Unless you're too scared?"

Arthur stood taller, puffing up his chest. "Not at all, *Albert*. I'm ready."

"I swear, Nikki and Grace could have had Frog planted by now," Charlie groaned, eyeing Grace mischievously. "Do we even need these guys?"

"Hey!" Leo huffed. "Mo and I aren't arguing! Are we, dude?"

Mo's cheeks lifted as he reached over to squeeze Leo's shoulder. "Nope," he said. "I think you're a delight."

Grace bit back her smile. "We are a *team*, Charlie," she said in her best Martha impression. "We are all equally important, lending our strengths in diverse ways. On one . . ." She stuck her hand out.

We all shuffled in annoyance to get our hands in place for our newly minted cheer.

"Two, three . . . *Go team!*" we whispered in unison.

"You have to admit, it's much more fun that way," Arthur said, squeezing by Mo to follow me, Mary, Bert, and Charlie out into the hallway.

"Don't get too comfortable," I warned him. "The fun's just starting."

Sticking close to the wall, the five of us moved quickly on our tiptoes toward the elevator bank.

I couldn't pinpoint the expansive feeling of warmth in my chest until I noticed our shadows grouped on the floor, passing over the linoleum like sneaky spirits.

All the other people in the world were walking around, living their lives, completely unaware that a mad scientist could release a lethal virus at any moment. I was worried about them, of course. Everyone deserved to be protected.

But it was the thought of losing my friends—my *family*—to something so awful that kept me moving that morning. Despite all their bickering, they still found time to take care of one another.

I could only hope I was moving toward a successful mission and not a dismal failure.

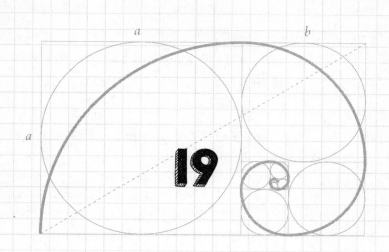

19

"Grace," I whispered into my GeckoDot. "How's that elevator coming?"

I peered out from the basket of laundry on wheels that Charlie had stashed me and Frog in. Arthur and Bert were fake-reading in the ward's waiting area, and Mary had stayed tucked silently in the corner of the room, pretending to write something in a journal.

There was a faint rustle, then Grace spoke. "We're having a bit of an *issue.*"

I scrunched my nose and shifted the towels above me, grappling for some fresh air. "What kind of an issue?"

"Er . . ." Grace responded. "It's the laptop . . ."

"Hold on, Nikki!" Mary said. My stomach lurched violently as the wheels of the laundry cart groaned and creaked underneath me. Wherever Mary was taking me, she moved fast. "Boys! Follow me!"

Quick footsteps and the squeak of sneakers followed us, and a dull *thud* made my whole body shake. A loud click followed, and finally, Mary's voice. "We're in the clear, Nikki. You can come out now."

I sprang from the laundry cart, flinging white sheets and thin towels into the air. "What's going on?!" I asked, whirling around. "Where are we?"

Sinks, urinals, and toilet stalls surrounded us, along with the faint whiff of industrial cleaner in the air.

"Oh, delightful," I said. "From a supply closet to a hamper to a bathroom. This day is full of surprises. What's the matter?"

"You heard Grace," Mary said through tight lips. "Leo's having a problem with the laptop." She glanced nervously at Arthur, who stood next to her, wringing his hands. He looked *guilty*.

"Well, he should be able to figure that out easily enough," I said. I set my hands on my hips. "Are you almost done, Leo?"

Mary and Arthur exchanged glances. Something wasn't right.

"Um . . ." Leo said. "It's not that simple. I need an outlet, but they're all near the nurses' station, so . . ."

Heat began to warm my cheeks. *An outlet?*

I turned to Arthur. "Did you . . ." I said, blinking fast. "Did you not charge the laptops, Arthur?"

One look at his creased eyebrows told me how badly he felt, and immediately, I regretted my tone. Any one of us could have made the mistake.

"I'm sorry," he said. "I did, I swear! But I think my older tech loses its charge a little faster than I realized, and . . . I guess I didn't leave them charging for long enough . . ." Arthur's cheeks burned red.

"It's okay, Artie," Mary said. "We can figure something else out." Her pinched expression didn't give me a lot of confidence.

Grace's voice in my ear confirmed my worst fears. "It's not looking good." Without Leo's laptop, we wouldn't be able to control the elevators . . . or nab the antidote.

It's seriously awful when plans go wrong. But it's even worse when they go wrong before you can even begin to implement them. A sudden flash of the pictures on Martha's phone during our first meeting blipped through my mind. People getting sick—*dying*, even, with nobody to protect them.

I imagined the airborne virus spreading around the earth. If my parents had stayed in Costa Rica after I had taken off, it might not reach them for a couple of days. But as travelers took to the skies, how long before the virus made its way all around the world?

We couldn't let a dead laptop stop us. Not even for a second.

"All right," I said, shaking my head to clear the awful images. "Let me get Frog going from here. We're running out of time, and whenever we *do* figure out how to control the elevator, we're going to need to be ready." I lifted the leather pack from my shoulder and set it gingerly in the laundry basket to unload the robot.

"All I need to do is turn it on and then . . ." I adjusted Frog's dart tube and pressed the small red button by his left foot.

Nothing.

"Um . . ." I said.

I hit the button again.

"What?" That was Charlie, following our actions from the hallway. "What is it, Nikki? Don't tell me it's not working either."

Bert smacked his forehead with his palm. "*It*," he exclaimed, "is yet another failure! I can't believe this! We're toast now! Arthur, does *any* of your stuff last longer than an hour?!"

I bared my teeth at Frog, ignoring the others. I absolutely refused to have *two* faulty pieces of tech ruin us before our plan got off the ground.

"Come on," I whispered to the robot. I smacked Frog's side, hoping a little percussive maintenance would spark it back to life. Something—*anything*—to indicate I could get it back working in time to use it. Arthur knelt beside me on the ground.

"Here." He reached out gently. "Let me?"

I sat back on my heels, hopeful that he'd have some nineteenth-century magic to use on our ancient robot. He cracked open the base and inspected Frog's insides. "This is the problem," he said, tapping one of the copper connections. "The wires are delicate. I think it must have fractured during transport."

The first threads of true panic started to worm their way into my chest.

"No," I said. I grabbed Frog from his hands and did my best to reposition the broken piece. "This can't be happening. It should be strong enough to withstand any little nudges in the pack." Setting the robot down again,

I bargained with the universe to give us one little win this morning.

But when I pushed Frog's on button again, there was still no flicker behind the robotic blue eyes.

I set the robot back into the laundry cart and wiped my hands on my jeans. Shaking my head at Mary, I made the call out loud so Grace could hear it. "It's no good," I said, resigned. "Frog's dead."

A shameful swell of fear constricted my throat.

Bert's freckles disappeared in the blush of his angry red face. Frog's death was a major blow to our plan. And Bert wasn't about to let Arthur off the hook for it.

"Without the laptop, we can't stop the elevator. Without Frog, we can't tranquilize the buyer or grab the antidote. Do you have *any* tech that works, Artie? Or was all of it built in the 1850s . . . and absolutely useless?!"

Arthur sniffed. "Well, if you hadn't been so preoccupied with bad-mouthing me at every turn, maybe you would have noticed that we'd been draining the batteries a little too much, and you could have offered some suggestions. It's not my fault that you weren't able to bring some of your own tech with you on this little adventure of yours!"

"Sure!" Bert yelled. "And if you'd leave your precious castle every so often, you'd know that modern devices like laptops need to be *charged* with something called electricity! You should try it sometime. It might liven up that old dump you live in. No wonder Frog died—it's as old as that ugly moth-eaten lump you call a sweater!"

Artie's nostrils flared. Apparently insulting his old-man sweater was a step too far. "You're just jealous that Mary brought you all here to *me* because you're completely useless at solving your own problems, *Albert.*"

"HA!" Bert's laugh was shrill. "If she cared about you that much, then how come she never told any of us about you! Even her best friend!" Bert jabbed his finger at me.

"Whoa." I leaped out of the way and held up Frog by my chest as a shield. "Don't drag me into this!"

"Oh, like you aren't thinking the same thing, Tesla!" Bert snapped.

I squeezed my eyes shut, wishing more than anything that Martha or Grace were in the bathroom with us. They'd know exactly how to stop this stupid bickering and get everyone's spirits up again. But Grace was busy trying to wrangle Bert's attention away from the anger that had gotten so intense he could barely listen. And Martha? I could only hope that those MI6 agents were treating her fairly in custody.

My biggest fear was playing out before my eyes.

And it wasn't the end of the world.

What I was most afraid of, though I hadn't realized until that very moment, was my team splintering apart. Genius Academy was self-destructing.

The government might have shut us down. But *we* were the ones letting our mission die. And in the chaos of the moment, with so many lives in the balance and evil villains chasing their victories, I had no way to stop it.

Luckily, someone else did.

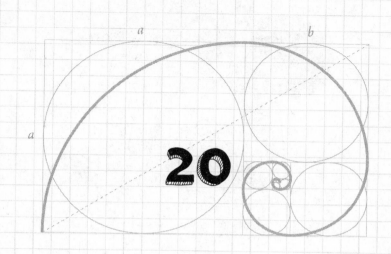

20

"ENOUGH!" Mary erupted.

She threw her hand up to block Bert and Arthur from getting any closer. "Both of you! You're acting like absolute idiots! Bert—it's not Artie's fault the laptop wasn't charged fully and Frog died. Accidents happen, and he didn't *ask* for us to bring him into our mission!"

"So much for deductive reasoning," Bert muttered under his breath. Mary glared daggers at him.

"And you!" She whirled around to face Arthur, who leaped back so quickly, he nearly tripped over me. "It's not Bert's fault that we needed help. We lost our home! We didn't come to you because we couldn't do it on our own—we came here because time is running out, and I *thought*"—she jabbed him in the chest with her

finger—"that you could put away your giant ego for five seconds to help someone other than yourself!"

An awkward wounded silence hung in the air. Both Bert and Arthur looked deflated.

Leo laughed easily in my ear, breaking the icy moment. "Cool! Well, now that that's settled, let's get back to our jobs."

I smiled gratefully. We needed to get ourselves back on track, and *fast*.

"Leo's right," I jumped in. "There are eight of us, a set of elevators we can't control, and a sedative dart we can't administer. How do we get that antidote?"

An uncomfortable silence followed as the four of us in the bathroom stared at each other.

"Come on!" Mo joined me. "This is what we do! We

solve problems! When was the last time something went easily, huh? Big whoop, our stuff died. So we find another way!"

Grace spoke next, her voice tinny over the GeckoDot. "We have to be able to stop the elevators. That's the only confined space in the building where we can get the buyer alone without too many variables. We cannot get caught, no matter what, because after our last escape, those agents won't underestimate us again. Agent Donnelly and his friends could be anywhere."

"If everything's electronic," Bert said, "then how can we control the elevators without a laptop? Even if we jam one of the motors somehow, we can't do it without physi-cally being there on the ground. Too easy to be caught."

"We could try to access it from the hospital's security desk?" Mo suggested.

"Too many witnesses," Grace pointed out.

"*This* is why I prefer my way of working," Arthur said, tucking a stray curl of hair behind his ear. "You call it old-school, but all these electronics are too easy to hijack! There's no way to stop an elevator remotely these days without tech."

"Well, for someone who doesn't like it, you've sure got a lot of robots," Bert mumbled. "Maybe that's why none of them work when it matters."

I gritted my teeth against Bert's negativity, urging myself to think through the problem. We'd tried our usual approach—hacking the elevators and staying out of sight. What was left if that didn't work? Was Arthur right? Was *old-school* a better way to get anything done? I didn't think so. But maybe . . .

"That's it!" I blurted. A fresh idea surprised me, zinging into my thoughts without notice. Excitement buzzed across my skin. "We don't need to *stop* the elevator," I said. I reached into my shoulder bag and dug around my ferret, searching for the solution I needed. "Sorry, Pickles, you can't come out just yet." She chattered back at me in anger.

Charlie answered. "Of course we need to stop the elevator. If we don't, how are we going to arrange for the knockout drug to be administered?"

I shook my head. "We can still do the knockout," I explained, still digging. I handed a pile of random items from the bag to Arthur, who watched me curiously. A bottle of water. Tissues. A pack of gum. A straw. Extra quarters.

"We wait until the antidote's in the elevator as planned, and then one of us administers the drug!"

"What do you mean 'one of us'?" Grace asked. "How? The robot is useless."

"We don't need it!" I glanced at Arthur, who already had a mischievous grin on his face. He knew exactly what I was thinking and held up the straw to prove it.

The others looked at me like I was cracking up from the pressure, but I knew I was onto something. "See, we don't need to control the elevator *if* we're already in there." I raced over to the bathroom sink and grabbed a paper towel, tearing away a tiny corner and popping it into my mouth. Chewing slowly, I drew more than one puzzled look from the others.

"Tesla, what are you—" Charlie started.

"This is how we do it!" I brought the straw to my mouth and spit the tiny wad of wet paper into it, turning my aim toward Bert.

He clued into my plan a moment too late.

"Don't you dare!" He lifted his hand to block me, but I let out a quick blow and the spitball shot through the air, landing squarely in the middle of his glasses with a *SPLAT.*

Mary clasped her hands together. "A blow dart!"

"Hold on." That was Leo now. "You want to use a blow dart to administer the drug and steal the antidote?"

Mary grinned excitedly. "It could work!"

"That's right," I said, grinning at her. "We do it old-school. One of us hides in the elevator, above the ceiling. When Victor's buyer steps inside, we use a blow dart to send the sedative down, they fall asleep, we've got ourselves a perfectly good antidote, and we haven't been caught. The rest of the plan stays the same. Only one of us is at risk, and the rest stay hidden."

They were all silent.

Bert reached up and plucked his glasses from his face, picking my goopy spit wad from his lens with a grossed-out grimace.

"Eww," he said, attempting, and failing, to flick it from his finger.

Arthur watched him with glee, his smile growing wider every second as Bert's disgust grew. "I don't know about you all," Arthur said, watching Bert wipe his fingers on the front of his pants. "But that's the best idea I've heard all day."

In our ears, Grace agreed with him. "You've sold me," she said. "Who wants to be in charge of the blow dart?"

Silence.

I scanned the possibilities in my head. Charlie was most athletic, so she'd be our best option. Or maybe Leo, because he was fastest in a pinch, in case he needed to move quickly. Even Grace, with her thin build and ability to talk herself out of every situation, might be a smart choice.

But then I realized that whoever was in that elevator with the antidote would also be closest to harm. That was the only variable I needed to know.

"I'll do it," I said quickly. I forced an easy smile on my face. "It was my idea, and I'd hate for one of *you* to get all the glory."

"We're all risking something here, Nikki," Mary said. She hadn't fallen for my false bravado. "You don't need to protect us."

"I'm not." I walked to the sink and bent over, turning on the faucets to let some cool water rush over my hands. "I actually got some practice with blow darts while I was in Costa Rica." I splashed my face, wanting to appear cool while angling my face away from Mary and Arthur, who would no doubt be able to smell my lie easily.

There'd been no blow-darting in Costa Rica. But if I was going to keep them away from that elevator, they'd have to believe me.

A peek at Arthur's quizzical expression in the reflection of the mirror told me that he didn't buy it. There really was nothing that got past him.

I pressed my lips together and tried to implore him telepathically. *Don't say a word.*

"Okay, Tesla," Grace said finally. "It's all yours. Leo is going to create a small diversion on the floor below so Nikki can get into the elevator shaft. Bert, you'll have to help her up."

"You can trust me," I said, swallowing my fears.

The truth was, I was worried about the buyer. I'd rather mud-wrestle a hippo than try to steal from a billionaire who'd let the whole world suffer from a deadly virus if it meant he'd make money on the cure, especially using only a straw and gravity. But I wasn't about to tell them that. This was our only choice.

"I'll get that antidote." I gave Mary a quick hug, snagged the small tranquilizer dart from Frog, and slipped it into my jacket pocket along with the straw. "Be ready to move on my signal."

"We'll be ready," Mary promised.

"And, Nikki?" Leo spoke in my ear again.

"Yeah?" I smiled at him, even though he was nowhere with us in the room. I wanted more than anything to give him a giant hug before I went up in that elevator, but I'd have to settle for his words in my ear.

"Don't miss," he said.

I laughed. "Wouldn't dream of it."

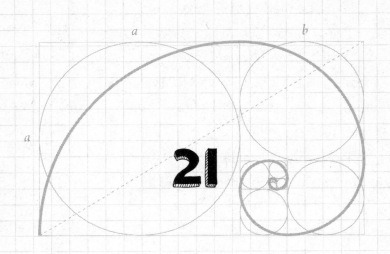

21

Take it from me: If you're claustrophobic, don't sneak into a dark elevator shaft in a creepy hospital that was founded in 1123. It does nothing for your nerves.

My insides were shaking like I was on my eighth cup of coffee. And I'd never even *tried* the stuff before, except for a sip from my mom's cup one morning. (Coffee is *terrible* and tastes like ground-up dirty socks, if you ask me.)

See? That's how you can tell how nervous I was.

I was *rambling*.

Shifting my weight, I hoisted myself up onto my elbow. Stretched out on my stomach with my head directly positioned above a small hole in the elevator ceiling, I'd had plenty of time to contemplate how on earth I'd ended up in this mess, and how much *bigger* of a mess we'd be in if I didn't get it right today.

One shot. One dart.

What if I blew it?

Like, *metaphorically*, I mean. You know, messed it up?

I'd inspected the tiny needle dart in my pocket, and it wasn't super strong. That was fine when Frog was going to be launching it with mechanical force. But my lungs weren't nearly as strong. What if whoever I was knocking out was wearing a thick jacket, and I couldn't pierce it? Or what if they happened to look up and noticed a random twelve-year-old girl peering down at them from the elevator ceiling like some sort of haunted gargoyle? They'd contact the police and all eight of us would get arrested again with zero hope of ever returning home.

My stomach clenched. Agent Donnelly would never let me out of his sight again. I wiped away a sniffle with the back of my hand. The dust in this place was no joke.

Oh God.

Another horrible image to worry about: What if I *sneezed* and accidentally blew the dart onto the floor and wasted it? Or accidentally stabbed myself and ended up knocked out above an elevator in a foreign country?! I'd have to explain to the others that the world was going to end because of allergies.

"How you doing there, Nik?" Leo's voice made me jump.

"Great!" I said, then immediately grimaced. I sounded way too excited to be telling the truth. "Fine," I amended. "It's fine. Totally cool up here. Tons of room, too."

Leo laughed. "Yeah, you sound really chill and under control."

"I just want to get this over with," I admitted. "It smells like something died."

"Well, it *is* a hospital," Bert replied, joining in the conversation in my ear. "I bet tons of people have died in this very building."

"We've got him!" Grace interrupted. "We've got eyes on Victor!"

I sucked in a breath, gripping the straw and blow dart in my left hand while angling myself toward the hole again. While Bert had helped get me into the elevator shaft, the rest of the team had stationed themselves around the entrances of the building, scanning for anyone who looked like Victor.

"Does he have it?" I hissed. "The antidote. Do you see it? Where are they?!"

The questions tumbled out of me. The last time we'd been around Victor, he'd *wanted* us to be there, and totally played us for fools. This time we had the element of surprise.

I wasn't going to waste it.

Grace continued to relay information. "Second floor," she said. "It's too early to tell if he's carrying anything. Could be in his jacket pocket maybe. If anyone's in a position to be caught, turn off your GeckoDot now."

I peeled the dot from my earlobe and stuck it to my forehead, so whatever Grace was recording from her point of view would be projected where I could see it.

A brief flicker blipped in front of me, then a crystal-clear holographic image of one of the hospital waiting areas appeared. A pile of magazines on a stark white table-top. A woman in blue scrubs, clutching a clipboard as she scurried past the elevator bank. Then, finally, a tall man in a plain white button-up shirt and black pants sat casually but kept peering around the room. Like he was waiting for someone. There was no doubt about it: It was Victor.

"That's him!" I confirmed. "Grace, how are you getting this without him seeing you?!" Instantly, my worries went from the rest of the team to Grace, who was clearly close enough to this bad guy to get such clear footage.

I heard the tiniest lilt of a laugh. "Don't worry about me," she said. "Mo gave me a makeover." She tilted her camera view toward herself, showing off a face nearly completely covered in gauze bandages. "It's the latest fashion. I call it Mummy After a Bad Fall. I look like a particularly unfortunate patient."

"Nice job, Mo," I said.

"Thanks," he whispered back. "We used about half the gauze in the supply closet, but she's totally pulling it off."

Grace's camera flipped back to Victor, and my eyes trained on the small envelope in his hand. There was definitely a lump—something tube-shaped, maybe—pressing against the paper sides.

His ankle bounced on his knee, and a flash of irritation tore through me. We were all working our butts off to stop him from ushering in a global catastrophe, and here he was looking so relaxed he might as well have been ordering a cheeseburger for lunch.

"Look!" I whispered, glaring at a man in dark glasses, a green polo shirt, and a Louis Vuitton messenger bag who'd appeared in the corner of the projected image.

"Could that be the guy who's buying the antidote?" I chewed anxiously on my lip, desperate to get out of here as quickly as possible. "He looks rich."

"That's not him," Arthur replied. "He's got a stuffed animal in that bag. He's waiting to see his kid. Probably had minor surgery. Tonsillitis, I bet."

I made a face. I'd forgotten that hanging out with Arthur and Mary basically meant you felt like an idiot at least half the time.

"Never mind," I muttered. I closed my eyes for a moment and imagined I was back in Costa Rica with my parents. It was becoming a habit now, finding some solace in their imaginary presence. Had Martha even had the chance to let them know about the mission before she'd been arrested? The list of things I'd need to apologize for was growing by the second.

"He's here!" Charlie's voice jerked me back to the present, and I refocused on the hologram in front of me.

Charlie was right. A man with tousled graying hair and a button-up shirt with khakis had sidled up to Victor, sitting opposite him in the waiting room. He glanced up expectantly, giving Victor the tiniest of nods.

"Something isn't right," Arthur said. "That can't be him."

A sharp edge of uncertainty cut through me. "What?"

I demanded. "What do you mean? That's obviously him, Arthur."

"It *can't* be," he said. "Look at that hair! A guy who can afford to buy a multi-billion-dollar biological agent can afford to get a haircut. And that shirt? You can see the plastic remnant from a department-store tag on the sleeve. There has to be someone else here . . ."

"So he bought a new shirt," Bert replied. "That doesn't mean he's innocent! It means he went shopping!"

My nails dug into my palm. Whatever was happening, I only had one dart, and one chance to get the right guy, or the whole mission failed.

"Grace, am I darting this guy or what? I need to know!"

Grace didn't hesitate. "Yes, dart him."

"No!" Arthur said. "It's not him! I know what you think you're seeing, but you're wrong. He's obviously here to trip us up."

I shook my head in frustration as I watched the scene play out before me. Grace was right: The man—the one Arthur was convinced *wasn't* the buyer—got up from his chair and sat right next to Victor. His hands fidgeted as they spoke briefly. He was clearly nervous and constantly checking over his shoulder.

"He's not acting like an innocent man," Mo pointed out. "Arthur, I think you're mistaken on this one, sorry."

My stomach turned as Victor reached into his inner jacket pocket and pulled out a thick envelope, passing it over quickly. "The exchange," I whispered. "It's happening! This *has* to be it!"

I strained to hear what the two men were saying, but Grace was too far away for any clear audio. Still, the picture gave us all the information we needed: Victor had passed along the envelope and accepted another package in return. What more was there to know?

"That's got to be the payment," I said. I bit the inside of my cheek and weighed what I was seeing. Arthur wasn't infallible. He was a genius, like the rest of us. But he was also human, and humans make mistakes all the time. I was certain of it: He was wrong on this one.

Which meant I had a job to do in about thirty seconds.

Charlie seemed to agree. "Nikki, he's heading to your elevator right now."

"Don't do it!" Arthur repeated. "Something isn't adding up here!"

Grace overruled him. "Our job isn't to catch the buyer, Arthur," she explained. "The *only* thing we care about is that antidote. This is where the exchange was supposed to happen. These two are the only men in the room exchanging *anything*—they're the only ones even talking to each other. We've got to move now while we have the chance."

My pulse slammed in my chest as the man stepped inside the elevator directly below me. My vision flickered slightly—I'd been holding my breath for too long while the others argued. I forced in a gulp of metallic air as quietly as I could.

I pressed the dot on my forehead once, turning off the GeckoDot's visuals. The team would still be able to hear me, but for now, I was the only one who could see what was going on below me.

Grace's voice was measured in my ear. "Bert is ready for you on the ground floor, Nikki."

I placed the dart in the straw and brought it to my

lips, readying myself to blow. Squinting one eye shut, I tried to imagine a giant target on the man's neck, impossible to miss.

Taking in one last breath, I wrapped my lips around the straw—now was the moment. Only a few seconds had passed since he'd stepped in the elevator. He'd pressed the ground-floor button once.

Now, I told myself.

A tinny ring made me nearly drop the straw right onto his head.

"What happened?" Bert whispered. "Did you do it? Nik?"

I didn't dare say a word.

The man was receiving a phone call.

I probably should have darted him right then, while he was distracted, and his neck craned ever so slightly to listen to the phone in his left hand. But that's when I noticed it: the tiny bit of plastic that Arthur had mentioned.

The price tag had been mostly torn away, leaving only a scrap and the plastic thread.

"Do you see, Nikki?" Arthur whispered. "Can't you see this isn't right? There are others that Victor could be working with here—"

A faint rustle sounded, followed by a thudding of feet, racing on the tiled floor.

"Arthur!" Grace said. She was angry now. *"Shh!"*

I burned through all of Arthur's arguments at warp speed in my mind, but every single one was knocked down easily by Grace's reasoning. The timing. The meeting. The exchange.

It was just the plastic tag of a new shirt.

He was the right guy. And if I hadn't been convinced of that, the next words out of the man's mouth told me everything I needed to know, as he talked with whoever was on the other end of that phone call.

"Yes," the man said. "I got it. The antidote is ours."

Thank you.

Certainty flooding my body, I dropped my face as low as I would dare to the hole in the elevator ceiling, bringing the straw to my mouth, and took aim. A patch of tanned skin stared up at me, above his shoulder and below his ear.

I blew out as hard as I could and watched as the dart zinged through the air, its small feather twisting like a glowing firefly, and lodged directly in the man's neck.

"Bert," I said, watching the man begin to sway slightly. "He's all yours."

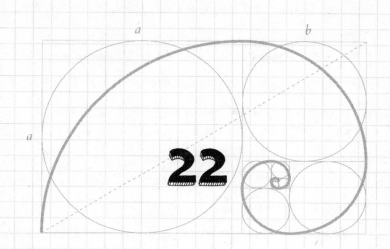

22

What do you do after you secretly drug a criminal and steal a billion-dollar, world-saving antidote from him?

Well, you run.

Everyone on the team had a job to do after our target collapsed. Bert snuck into the elevator, hitting the emergency stop and halting it between floors to grab the package from the target's backpack, along with his wallet to find out his identity. I dropped down from the ceiling like an awkward spider monkey and helped Bert while the others staggered their exits from the hospital so as not to arouse any suspicion.

Our plan was to meet in the back corner of a local café, a quick tube trip away from the hospital. Bert and I were the last to arrive, and my knees still shook with nerves as I collapsed into the chair that Leo shoved out for me.

"You did it!" he exclaimed. He gripped my shoulders in both hands and scrutinized me, then planted a kiss on my cheek. "Are you okay? Did you get hurt at all?"

I blushed, painfully aware that the others were watching us. "I'm fine!" I replied. "Everything went well. It was almost . . ."

"Easy?" Bert offered.

"Almost *too* easy," Arthur said. A troubled expression clouded his face. "Listen, I know that you don't believe me, so—"

Bert laughed, still a little giddy from our success. "Aww, Artie, don't feel too bad for being wrong on this one," he said. He held up his bag with the antidote in it and waved it happily. Even Arthur couldn't dampen his spirits now. "Nobody's right all the time. Shall we celebrate? Donuts on me!" He handed the bag to Grace and rubbed his hands together, heading over to the counter, where a row of pastries was displayed. I had to admit, the promise of sugar and fried dough made the whole day seem a little brighter. I couldn't even remember the last time we'd actually finished a proper meal.

Grace cleared a spot on our table and set the bag down, carefully opening the flap to pull out the envelope.

"Should we really open that thing in here?" Charlie asked, edging away from her.

"It's not radioactive," Grace said. She pulled out the thick envelope and held it to the light. "But we need to be certain it's the antidote before we find a way to get in touch with Martha again. With this as proof of what's going on, she can explain why we were at the Tower and prove our innocence, and they'll release her by the end of the day." She gingerly lifted one end of the envelope and let the contents tip slowly out onto the table.

I don't know what I was preparing to see. A bubbling vial of green potion? A metal canister with a high-tech dial lock? What did antidotes even look like?

It turns out they look a lot like candy.

Seriously. The envelope contained a transparent

tube. But inside the tube, instead of the serum or liquid I was expecting to see, a row of multicolored tablets was stacked in the glass, with a black metal stopper on the top.

"Huh." Grace frowned, touching the tube lightly with her finger to test for temperature before picking it up. She held it over the table for us to see. "Do we have any information about what *type* of antidote this is? I was expecting some sort of liquid. These look like . . . pills?"

Bert shrugged, still smiling. "So it's an oral medication, then, like headache tablets or vitamins." He glanced toward Arthur. "Chemists will have no problem breaking down the components. They could use this to manufacture enough for anyone infected by the Spark virus."

"Can I see them?" Mary reached out her hand.

Grace passed her the tube while Charlie dragged her chair over to sit beside Mary.

"I don't know," Charlie said. "Looks like sweets to me."

"Me too," I admitted. A flash of inspiration made me sit up in my chair. "It's camouflage!" I said. I grabbed the tube from Mary and grinned. "I bet they only look like candy to prevent rival manufacturers from stealing the formula. It's the perfect disguise. There's even little letters on them!"

As soon as the words escaped me, my throat clenched with panic.

Seven letters branded on the sides of the tablets, all in a row in the beaker.

"What?" Bert asked. "Tesla, what is it?"

Angry tears threatened to spill from my eyes. Arthur cleared his throat, and from the corner of my vision, he dropped his head in resignation.

"I tried to tell you all," he said quietly. He pushed his chair out from the table and walked over to where I was sitting. Still in shock, I passed him the tube so he could break the news to everyone. I couldn't bear to say it out loud.

He'd been right all along. He probably even knew what those tiny letters spelled out.

"You've got to be kidding me," Charlie cried. "Is it *not* the antidote?! Did we do all of that for nothing?!"

Arthur glanced sadly at Mary before popping the stopper from the tube with his left hand.

"Whoa!" Grace yelped. "What are you doing?! Don't contaminate them! We won't know what they are until a lab runs some tests!"

He ignored her, pouring the tablets out onto the

table in a long line. "I tried to tell you," Arthur repeated. He spaced out each of the tablets so we could easily read the letter on each.

"*N-I-C-E-T-R-Y.*" Mary read aloud. Upon reading the *Y*, her hand flew to her mouth, like she could stop the words from being real.

But it was too late.

"They don't *look like* candy," Arthur explained. "They *are* candy. Watch." Before we could stop him, he popped one into his mouth and began chewing loudly.

"Dude!" Mo shouted. "You can't just eat it!" His face fell. "Wait. Is it really candy?"

Arthur reached down and picked up another piece, this time taking a small bite from it with his front teeth. He held up the remaining part so we could see the inside. "Chocolate-covered peanuts," he said. "See?" Breaking the piece apart with his fingers, he scattered the messy bits on the table.

Grace buried her face in her hands.

"What does this mean?" Charlie asked. She twisted the tip of her ponytail with her fingers anxiously. "What do we do now?"

Nobody had the heart to say it. Charlie was a genius like the rest of us. She knew exactly what this meant.

We'd been set up *again*.

We'd wasted precious time tracking down a criminal and enacting a dangerous mission to extract chocolate-covered bleeping peanuts.

Bert was the first to speak. "It means we're doomed, Charlie." He glanced around the café and out the big bay window at the front of the room, with a flicker of new-found awe on his face. A little girl walked with her mother out on the street. Her tiny hand was stretched above her head, holding tight to her mom's pinky finger.

It was easy to take life for granted when you didn't know about the scary parts.

Bert set down his donut. "Deeply and utterly doomed."

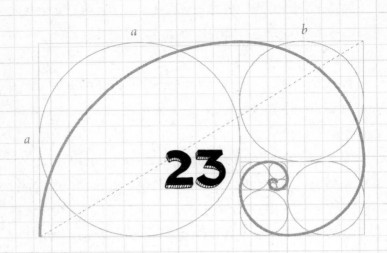

23

A deadened silence hung in the air as the pieces of the puzzle began to come together.

We'd been duped twice. First Victor had left us a note when he'd caused the explosion and diamond theft at the Tower of London. Now the candy was yet another taunting message.

He'd planned for us to track him down at the hospital and steal the fake antidote, just to rub it in our faces.

Why? Ordinary villains are cold. They like to show off their skills and genius, but they don't *create* situations just to mess with their pursuers.

This felt different. Personal.

My thoughts returned to Arthur's folder and the list of

science organizations that Victor was stealing money from. What was the connection?

Charlie looked around at the others with huge, sad eyes. "How are we going to get Martha back now?"

"It's not Martha we need to be worried about," Mo whispered. "Without the antidote, we're no closer to stopping the virus . . ." His eyes were wet.

"If I may," Arthur said. "I've got to tell you—"

"*Ugh,*" Bert interrupted. "Not *now*, Arthur. We get it, okay? You were right! We made the wrong call, and you were right all along! The stupid"—he gestured madly, sputtering out the words—"stupid *plastic tag* was all the information you needed. Isn't that right, oh, brilliant one?! We should have listened to you from the start!"

Arthur's mouth clamped shut, looking hurt. "I'm not trying to rub it in, Bert. But I may have a solution to your problem."

Bert sneered. "It's going to be *everyone's* problem pretty soon if Victor has his way. Unless you've got a way to get the antidote, maybe it's best if we just accept the fact that we blew it."

I wanted to jump in and defend Arthur. It wasn't his fault we'd messed up. In fact, he'd tried his best to help us. But my mouth felt like cotton. I had no idea what to say or how to make anything right.

Arthur swept the candy on the table into a pile and sat down again. He reached into his pocket. "I don't know how to find the antidote," he said. "But we don't need it."

"And why's that?" Grace asked, her shoulders sunk in resignation. Seeing her so defeated was almost as bad as feeling that way myself.

"What's the one thing that would be even better than getting our hands on the antidote?" Arthur asked.

Bert lifted a finger, a wry expression on his face. "Going back in time to stop the virus from being invented. Don't tell me you've got a time machine in that castle of yours."

"Or getting a hold of the Spark virus *itself*," Arthur said. "All this time we've been trying to get the antidote. But if we could neutralize the virus—stop it from ever being released in the first place—we wouldn't even need an antidote."

The café seemed to grow silent, as though even the pastries and espresso machines were listening intently to Arthur's idea.

"Sure," Mo said. "That would be great. But we're not exactly any closer to the virus than we were to the antidote."

"That's where you're wrong," Arthur said. His face

brightened. "While everyone was focusing on the man in the elevator, I paid attention to what was really happening," he explained. "After what you told me went down at the Tower of London, it seemed like Victor would be the type to want to actually *see* you guys mess up. He'd want to watch it happen. So I threw on some bandages like Grace and kept my eyes peeled for anyone who could be watching us as we made all our mistakes."

"Dude," Leo said. "You were doing all that while we were running our mission?"

"I know," Arthur said, looking down at his feet. "I should have told you all. But it was clear you weren't going to believe me. And I don't blame you. I'm not the best communicator. And all my tech failed you. So I thought it would be best to work by myself, in case I turned up empty-handed."

I gaped at Arthur, completely overwhelmed by his admissions. We were supposed to be geniuses—people who didn't miss anything. And somehow we'd been completely oblivious while one of our teammates carried out his own operation right under our noses.

Anger hit me first, but guilt and shame followed right at its heels.

"Oh, Arthur." Mary spoke first, voicing exactly what I

was feeling. "I'm sorry. We should have listened. We could have formed two teams, or backed you up so you weren't trying to do it all on your own. That's what Genius Academy does!"

His smile was sad. "You know I'm not part of Genius Academy," he said quietly. "But either way, I think I have a way to get what we really need here. I grabbed something at the hospital. From the most suspicious person in that waiting room."

Grace's eyebrows scrunched together. "Victor?" she asked. "We were watching him the whole time."

Arthur shook his head. He pulled a phone from his pocket and carefully punched in a four-digit code.

"I took this from a nurse at the hospital. Or someone dressed up as a nurse." He held up the screen. "Look at the phone contacts. *This* is your Victor, right?"

"That's him," I confirmed, pacing at the table.

"But his name isn't Victor," Arthur said. "See? It's Robert Walton. He's not in charge of anything. He's hired help. A diversion, in both the Tower and the hospital. The messages here confirm he was working for someone else. He was to appear as Victor and draw us in each time."

"Wait a second," Mary said. She wrapped her arms around her chest, like she was warding off a sudden chill. "Who did you take the phone from?" Her cheeks grew pale. "How on earth did you know the code?"

Bert scoffed. "That's obvious, isn't it? He *deduced* it." A glimmer of admiration appeared on his face.

But Arthur refused to acknowledge the compliment. "I didn't need to. The *V* from your original intelligence wasn't for Victor. Neither was my bank robber named Victor—I was wrong, too. There was only one suspicious person at the hospital that made any sense as our villain. And I recognized her right away."

"You're lying," Mary snapped. "It can't be."

Whatever she had sorted out in her mind was still a cloudy mess to the rest of us.

"What are you saying?" I asked. "Who are we dealing with?"

"Remember back in my lab?" he said, his eyes dark and unreadable. "You asked me what possible common thread there was between me and Genius Academy."

"Okay . . ." I said. Something about the sad expression on his face made my stomach clench with fear.

He handed me the phone. I pressed a button to turn on the screen, but the lock screen appeared again. An alphabetical display stared up at me, teasing with its infinite possibilities.

"The code?" I asked.

"The common thread," he said. "The thing connecting your mission—the reason you're here—and the person I've been tracking. It's *M*," he started. "*A-R-Y.*"

My hand hovered over the *Y* on the screen as I realized what I was typing. On my right, Charlie gasped.

"I pickpocketed the phone from her bag, Mary," he said quickly. "I was right there, and I saw her."

"Her? Victor is a *woman*?!" Mo said.

Arthur nodded, keeping his eyes locked on Mary. "Victor is Victoria."

"Who is she, Mary?" I asked. "And why is your name the code to her phone?" Arthur's words came back to haunt me. *There are no coincidences.*

She didn't answer. And by the numb look on her face, I wasn't sure that she'd even heard me.

"Are you going to tell them, Mary?" Arthur asked. "Or should I?"

Mary licked her lips, suddenly looking nervous. Pickles instinctively recognized her fear and raced over to her, attempting to snuggle with her fingertips.

"Victoria Wollstonecraft," she said. "That's who's behind the Spark virus."

"Wollstonecraft, as in . . . ?" Bert's mouth hung open at his words. "You're related?"

Mary ran her fingers through the fur on Pickles's neck absently, rocking ever so slightly back and forth in her chair. Her attention was fixed on something far away from any of us.

"As in . . . my mother's sister," she replied. "Victoria is my aunt."

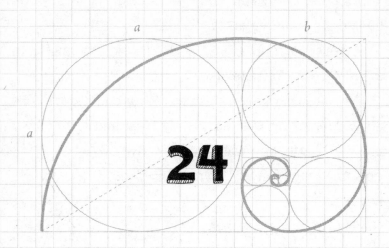

Up until this trip, I'd thought I knew everything about Mary.

I'd seen her happy, determined, annoyed, and even stubborn. But I'd never seen her truly terrified, not even when she'd been kidnapped by rogue mercenaries last year.

Today, that all changed.

Her chin trembled and her eyes glistened as she peered up at Arthur. I couldn't stand the sight of her so fearful, and already my blood pressure was rising, causing a dull roar in the corners of my mind.

In a blink, the entire team crowded around her. Bert was closest, resting his hand protectively on her shoulder while Arthur and the others shifted, unconsciously forming a ring around her to shield her from the rest of the café.

"I can't believe I missed it," Mary said finally. "I thought I saw her at the Tower. But . . . it was so fast." She licked her lips. "I didn't think it was possible. How could I have been so stupid?!"

Arthur dipped his head, as though the mention of Mary's aunt alone warranted a moment of grave silence.

I knew Mary had stayed with extended family when her parents had passed away all those years ago. I'd always wanted to ask her about it, but somehow, the moment never seemed right. She was always so sad when the topic of her parents came up, and what kind of a friend wants to make someone relive pain like that?

"Hey, maybe we should move this someplace else?" I urged, giving Grace a meaningful look. It was true that we needed answers, but there had to be a gentler way to get them.

But Mary held up her hand to cut me off. "No, it's all right, Nikki. I've already wasted too much of everyone's time with this." Her sniffles became full-blown tears dripping down her face.

This, of course, made me leap to her side. "None of this is your fault! You had no idea that you knew this person! Remember when *my* father was behind our last mission, and I didn't even know he was alive!" I kept my voice light and glared at Bert for help.

"Yeah," Bert jumped in. "Remember that time I dropped plutonium in the lab, and the only reason we didn't all die horrible deaths was because Leo caught it with his very weird but very useful catlike reflexes?!"

Leo nodded earnestly. "Or the time I set fire to the kitchen trying to figure out how to make a rocket thruster?"

"And let's not forget the death ray I made that nearly destroyed the world," I added with a grimace. "This was before you even *knew* me. And you were there for me right from the start."

Arthur nudged me. "Jeez, has your team ever *not* nearly caused global catastrophes?"

"That's totally beside the point, Artie," Bert said.

"But this isn't *like* that!" Mary sobbed. "I'm supposed to be the one who knows what's going to happen! I'm supposed to be able to read people. What good am I if I can't even see what's right in front of me?! You all do your jobs, and I totally failed at mine. I can't believe that people are going to *die* because I was too blind to see Aunt Victoria was to blame. I am *never* going to forgive myself!"

Grace's tone was gentle but firm. "Do you want to tell us what you know about her, Mary? That'd help inform what we do next."

I marveled at how Grace navigated such a sticky emotional situation, showing the perfect blend of caring and empathy for her friend while still remaining deeply logical. She knew we'd need answers, and soon, if we were going to stop Mary's aunt. I'd never been happier to have Grace on our team.

Mary sniffled again as Bert offered the sleeve of his shirt for her to wipe her tears. "It all makes sense," she said, throwing up her hands in frustration. "I should have seen it! She was a brilliant doctor when I knew her. And obsessed with mortality."

I glanced nervously at Arthur.

"I was taken away from her because she got into trouble," Mary continued. "*Serious* trouble. She was working on a way to . . ." Her voice choked.

"To what?" I urged her to go on. "It's okay, Mary. We've heard it all, you know that. What was she trying to do?"

Mary wiped her nose again, and tears continued to stream down her cheeks. "She was working on a way to reanimate the dead."

A hush fell over the group.

Maybe we *hadn't* heard it all.

One look at Mary's pained face and we all became desperate to make her feel better.

"That's it?" Bert coughed loudly. His act fooled no one, but he was kind enough to try for Mary's sake. "That's not so bad!"

"Yeah!" Charlie added, grinning widely. "We've seen worse before breakfast, haven't we, guys?! Who *hasn't* tried to bring back the dead, huh? Pretty sure Martha even had a class on that at the Academy back in the old days!"

A small smile tilted the corners of Mary's mouth. We were being ridiculous. She knew that. But it was enough to get a half-hearted laugh out of her.

"It's true, Mary!" Leo joined in. "Plus zombies and ghosts and the living dead are all the rage right now. Your aunt is on-trend!"

"You're way too forgiving," Mary said. Then she took a deep breath and began to tell us about her aunt. "Victoria was always performing illegal experiments— autopsies, research on tissue regeneration, you name it. She was a brilliant scientist." Mary stared at her hands while she spoke. "But I didn't understand as a child. One day, I came home from school and the house was empty. She said she'd be home, and when she wasn't, I got scared. So I ran to the neighbors for help. The Franklins were a sour old couple—always glaring at us and poking around our property like they thought Victoria was too smart for her own good. I hated them! But when she disappeared, I had nowhere else to turn. And soon after, the police arrived and told me that I'd be moving to foster care. I guess they went inside our house to look for her and found her laboratory."

I reached for her shoulder again. "Oh, Mary, that's awful. I'm so sorry."

Mary sniffled. "That's not the worst of it."

"What happened then?" Charlie asked.

"A fire," Mary choked out. "I stayed with the Franklins while the cops searched the house. But while I was at

the police station later that evening, I heard that before Victoria was arrested, she set fire to her laboratory. The police were talking all about it."

Nobody spoke, riveted by the images that Mary was conjuring with her story. How had she never told me any of this?

"Martha found me shortly after," she continued. "The last I heard, Victoria was in jail and had lost her license to practice medicine. But I guess she must have escaped—I can't imagine the authorities would have let her out on good behavior. And there's no way she could have come up with the Spark serum behind bars."

Grace tilted her head. "Do you have any idea why she would make something like that? Why a virus?"

Mary frowned. "She wasn't the type to want to hurt people. At least, not billions of them. She always told me she wanted to bottle the essence of life."

"The *spark* of life," Leo said, snapping his fingers. "That makes sense!"

"Or spark of a fire . . ." Bert said darkly. "Maybe she was trying to develop something that gave people a kind of superstrength that would allow them to defy illness or injury . . . to defy death! Only the whole thing blew up in her face, and it turned out to be lethal and not helpful?"

I turned over the possibilities in my head. "But that doesn't explain why she would create this elaborate *game* to tease us with it. We've also got Arthur's side of this— she's been stealing money from scientific organizations. Probably to fund her research. What are we missing here? Why would she bring Mary into any of this? Mary wouldn't hurt a fly, and Victoria must know it from her time with her." I turned to Mary, unsure of how to phrase my next question tactfully. I'd be a monster if I made her cry again.

"Was your aunt, *er* . . . someone who would ever turn on people?" I tried. "Like, would you put it past her to completely snap and want to, uh, destroy humanity?"

"Nice one, Tesla," Grace gave me a look. "Real smooth."

"Well, sorry!" I said. "But she knows what I'm trying to say here!" I leaned closer to Mary.

Mary chuckled sadly. "It's okay, Grace," she said. "I know how this works. You all need to know if my aunt was bananas. The truth is, I don't know. Maybe she blames the whole scientific community for being sent to jail? That could explain why she targets them in her robberies. And the serum itself would certainly do a number on a world that condemned her research. As for me?" Her eyes cast downward as she shrugged. "I don't know why she'd involve me at all. She might be angry that I accidentally got her arrested, I suppose. But I was so young . . . Maybe she wanted to keep us out of the way. If we hadn't escaped, we'd probably still be locked up with those British intelligence agents right now, unable to stop her."

I considered that. It seemed impossible that someone

related to Mary—the sweetest, kindest person alive—
would ever want to hurt anyone.

But families can surprise us. I knew that best of all.

"Was there anything else on the phone that might be
useful, Artie?" Mary looked up at him.

"I'm glad you asked," he said. "Your aunt kept very
clear records, Mary. We might not have the antidote, but
her plan to release the serum is all here. It can be released
into the air *or* someone's bloodstream, right?"

"Wait a second," Leo said, waving his hands in protest. "You're telling me that she left notes on her phone on
precisely how she was planning to release the virus?
That's way too easy! This has to be a trap. *Another* one so
she can outsmart us again."

Arthur crossed his arms. "Oh, it is definitely a trap. If
I hadn't pickpocketed her phone, I have a feeling she
would have handed it right to me. But I still think we need
to go. If history tells us anything, she *will* be there. I
wouldn't be surprised if she's enjoying having an audi-
ence. Plus, it's our last chance to get within ten feet of the
Spark serum. Maybe Mary can reason with her?"

Now it was my time to argue. "You want Mary to *reason* with this madwoman? After everything her aunt's put
her through?"

Arthur blushed, but Mary came to his aid. "I have

as much right to be there as the rest of you!" she said. "Besides, Arthur's right. We've come this far. For some reason, Victoria seems bent on keeping us just out of reach. We have to go, and we have to do everything we can to stop her from releasing the Spark serum." Her meaning was clear. "And I mean *everything*."

I had to speak up, even though the logic of Mary's plan made sense. "I really don't think you should go anywhere near Victoria," I said. "It's too dangerous. She's clearly wrapped you up with this chaos in her mind, and what if . . ."

I couldn't finish my thought. It was too awful.

The team turned to Grace, who had been silent as she watched us all carry on.

"What's it to be, G?" Bert asked.

For the first time, I wasn't sure *what* I was hoping to hear. Part of me wanted Grace to say that there was no way we were going to do exactly what Victoria wanted. That it would obviously blow up in our faces and that we'd be stupid to do it.

But the other part? The reckless part that hated to see my best friend in such pain and despised *anyone* who would play with humanity like this, that part of me wanted to set things right.

Maybe even more, that part of me wanted *revenge*.

What Arthur had said was true: This was our last chance to grab the Spark serum before Victoria unleashed it. I didn't know how we'd manage to get it out from under her. But all other outcomes were unthinkable.

Which is how I knew what Grace was going to say before she said it. When it came to Genius Academy, saving the world was important because that was how we saved each other. Maybe Mary and Arthur weren't the only ones who could predict the future.

"I say we do it," Grace said. She reached down and grabbed one of the chocolate-covered peanuts from the table and popped it into her mouth, chewing slowly. "But this time, we don't mess it up. She knows we're coming. So we need to *act* like she knows."

The rest of us were silent, but the resolve in my chest was growing by the second. We were walking into a trap, and we knew it.

"So," Leo said casually. "Where is she planning on releasing the serum? Tell me we get to go home soon?"

My shoulders clenched. Where would the virus do the most damage? It had to be someplace public. Somewhere big and busy and full of people, where the Spark of Life would spread at a rate that was impossible to stop.

Arthur turned the phone in his hand to show us the

screen. A picture of a beautifully designed transparent pyramid stared back at us. "Paris," he said. "At midnight tomorrow, she's going to use an aerosol system to contaminate a highly trafficked tourist attraction before it fills to capacity in the morning. And she's chosen a famous piece of art as her target."

I winced.

I hate being right all the time.

"The Venus de Milo," Arthur continued. "Ever been to the Louvre?"

It should have ended there. We should have calmly finished our donuts, cracked through our plan together, and booked tickets to Paris, France, so we could figure out a way to sneak into the world's most famous museum before Mary's aunt went full mad scientist on the global population.

But if you've learned anything from these records—or from my *life*— it's that nothing ever goes the way it should.

I had a bite of warm, raspberry-filled donut in my mouth when it happened. The taste and aroma of sugar and berries were strong, and for a brief moment, I was able to clear my head from the day's disasters.

And then—

"Nikola Tesla!" A booming voice cut through my donut reverie. Around me, the others had already begun to shove their chairs away from the table.

I whipped around, still holding the donut in one hand. Pickles clawed her way up my other arm, digging her nails into my skin. The café customers jumped at the noise, their dishes and cups clattering to the floor as a group of tall men in rumpled suits rushed toward us.

Through the chaos, I caught sight of a square jaw attached to a *very* ticked-off member of MI6.

Agent Donnelly.

You've got to be kidding me.

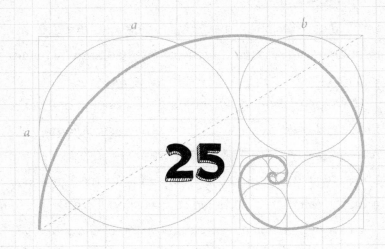

There are three things that every wanted criminal under-stands before entering a room:

1) Never, *ever* sit with your back to the entrance.
2) Don't let anyone corner you without an escape.
3) Always, without fail, know your exits.

Unfortunately for me, Mary's crying had made me forget numbers one and two. When Agent Donnelly crashed into the café with two other agents, I didn't even see him, and I was completely cornered, with my back tucked next to the pastry counter and cash register.

Unfortunately for Agent Donnelly, I hadn't forgotten rule number three.

"Scramble!" Grace bellowed, kicking the table and throwing her mug in the direction of the agents.

Donnelly dodged the flying cocoa but tripped on the corner of one of the other tables as he lunged to grab her.

Twenty seconds ago, the eight of us had been crowded around a single table. Now only four of us remained; Bert, Mo, Charlie, and Grace had all weaseled their way down into the basement, or out through a back window in the men's bathroom. I'd always thought my team's greatest skill was our mental genius, but I was beginning to realize that our ability to scatter from police was at near-Olympic levels.

"Don't even think about it, Nikola," Agent Donnelly said to me. He wasn't holding a gun, but he continued to edge his way toward me slowly with his arms outstretched. I gritted my teeth as I noticed the bloom of a bruise on his temple.

Oops. That would be my fault.

I widened my arms as though to block the others from view. Mary, Arthur, and Leo shifted instinctively behind me. Cracked and broken pieces of ceramic mugs and glassware crunched beneath my feet as we moved, and my breath came out in sharp pants.

"I'm sorry," I said, gesturing to his hand. "But we can't come with you. Not yet."

Agent Donnelly's eyes widened with incredulity. He still wasn't used to being told no. But being told no by a kid was clearly too much for him.

"Excuse me?!" he sputtered. "You're all coming with me right now!"

"We can't!" I shouted. "Don't you get it? We're on the same side. We didn't blow up the Tower of London. Besides, this situation is so much bigger than that. And all you're doing is getting in the way. You *have* to let us go. There's no time to waste!"

To my surprise, the angry lines on Agent Donnelly's face disappeared. He held up his hand, gesturing to his fellow agents to freeze.

"Tell me, then," he said. "Tell me exactly what you're doing here, Nikola. You've got three seconds before I arrest you again. Convince me that you and I aren't enemies."

I swallowed hard, feeling the stares of Leo, Mary, and Arthur on my back. Should I tell him? Maybe he could actually help us. Having police backup at the museum could be the thing that tipped the scales in our favor for once. And he really did seem sincere in wanting to know what we were doing.

"Well . . ." I began. Instead of Agent Donnelly's face, it was Martha's that swam in front of me. She'd been very clear from the start. Agents had died because of what they knew. Mary's hand reaching for mine confirmed my thoughts.

"Nikki, no," she whispered.

"I can't!" I yelled to Agent Donnelly. "You've got to trust me! We're trying to stop a global catastrophe here, all right?! I'm only trying to protect you!"

He gawked at me like I'd told a bad joke. "Protect *me*?" He laughed. "Mate, I don't know who you think you are, but you're going to explain everything to me. At headquarters. *Now.*"

I stepped back again, shifting on my toes. A slight breeze from the back room tickled my ankle. Someone—Grace probably—had left a window open or broken it entirely.

"Nope," I said. "Not going to happen." I forced a grin on my face. If I couldn't convince Agent Donnelly that we were on the same side, then I'd have to try another tactic.

I'd have to get him angry enough that he'd make a mistake.

Angry enough to distract him for *one second*.

"Why don't you grab a donut and relax for a minute?" I pointed to the counter, where a very scared and confused barista shot her hands in the air. "You look tired."

A muscle in his jaw jumped. He took another step closer, trying to corral us against the wall. "Enough games," he muttered. He reached behind his back and pulled out a set of handcuffs. "You're coming with me."

"Arthur . . ." I had no idea if the others were still behind me, but the crunch of glass under my feet continued. They wouldn't have all left me like that.

"I'm here," Arthur said.

"Now would be a good time for that party we were talking about," I said between clenched teeth.

"Way ahead of you," he answered.

I pinched my lips together hard and held my hands up in apology. "It's nothing personal," I told Agent Donnelly, shifting quickly to the left so Arthur had a wide berth to throw his balloon grenade between me and the wall, aiming at the agent's feet.

Donnelly yelled something, but whatever he said was drowned out by the explosion of glitter paint all over the café.

Say what you will about Arthur's ancient tech, there was definitely a time and place for a good old-fashioned glitter bomb, and that time and place was in this café, with three *very* ticked-off agents hunting us down. Operation Disco Ball—inspired by Bert—hadn't been our plan, but it had worked perfectly.

Huge splatters of paint shot through the air, and though I'd never seen unicorn vomit, I imagined it looked something like the mess of hot-pink and blue sparkles that covered the walls, the agents, and ourselves.

With the agents cursing and disoriented, the four of us had the chance we needed. We turned on our heels and bolted for the back room. I'd been right about the window in the men's bathroom—and thanks to the others, it was still hanging open, damaged on its left hinge.

With Arthur and Leo's help, I hoisted Mary up and out the window, then took Leo's hand as we hopped out after her, with Arthur following right behind us.

"Where are we going?" Arthur panted after us. My legs burned with exertion as we pounded up the pavement as fast as we could, skidding around corners and through alleyways. Agent Donnelly and his men had been prepared, but they'd made one crucial mistake: They'd assumed we'd be leaving with them out the front door and had nobody stationed at the back. Grown-ups really did underestimate kids all the time.

"Paris!" Mary answered.

I know I should have been too focused to notice, but a tiny part of my heart jumped to see her reach out and grab Arthur's hand. Maybe she was only trying to get him to speed up, but still. So sweet, right?

"We need to lose these agents," Leo said.

"Wait!" Arthur came to a quick stop, causing Mary to smash into him.

"What are you doing?!" she yelled. "Keep going! We need to put more ground between us!"

"No, look!" Arthur said, doubling over. He stretched out an arm to point at the side of the alleyway where a pair of motorcycles sat waiting.

"Well, that's convenient," Leo said.

"Really, guys?" I said. "You want to steal some bikes? I don't even know how to ride these things! Quit messing around!" I turned on my heel, but Mary grabbed my arm.

"You don't need to," she said. "*We* do. Isn't that right, Leo?"

Leo's shoulders lifted to a shrug, but he couldn't hide the smirk on his face. "They're nice bikes," he mused. "Four helmets, too. It's almost too good to pass up. Be a lot quicker than running."

"Sure," I said, rolling my eyes. "And totally illegal."

"You stole a private plane last year," Mary reminded me. She dragged me over to one of the motorcycles and grabbed the helmets from the back. Handing me one, she spoke quickly. "Look, they were naive enough to leave the keys in the helmets. It's meant to be. Put this on. You're coming with me. Leo, you take Arthur."

"Done," Leo said, tossing Arthur a helmet from his own motorcycle.

"Shouldn't I go with Mary?" Arthur asked timidly. "I mean, if we're splitting up into teams here?"

"Why, so we can pair up boy-girl like they do in the movies and ride off into the sunset?" Mary sniffed.

She swung her leg over the motorcycle and turned the ignition. "Not interested. Nikki and I need some girl talk. You boys can take care of yourselves. The others will be headed to the Louvre, I'm sure of it. We can hide out in the gardens there and figure out our next move when we all reconnect."

Swelling with pride at Mary's sudden confidence, I put on the helmet and joined her on the motorcycle, clinging to her jacket. "You heard the woman," I said. "Last one there is wanted for grand theft auto!"

The engine growled under us as Mary gripped the throttle, sending our chopper roaring to life. Hanging on

for dear life, I prayed to whatever motorcycle gods existed for a safe trip. We zipped down Gower Street in King's Cross, weaving our way through packed London traffic toward St Pancras train station.

It was no romantic trip into the sunset, but given the week I'd had, I was going to have to take what I could get.

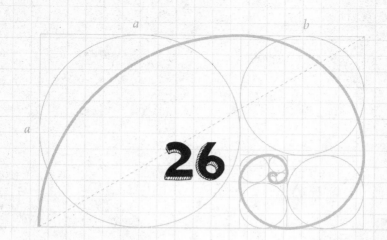

I had to hand it to the French; the gardens outside the Louvre were the nicest I'd ever seen.

Officially called the Tuileries and Carrousel Gardens, they were the perfect place to have a picnic, people watch, and enjoy the buzzing bees, trees, and a rainbow of flowers as a perfect warm breeze drifted through the air.

They were also a great place to meet up with your exhausted team and plan a last-ditch effort to save the world.

After taking a train through the tunnel under the English Channel to France (paid for by Arthur), we'd grabbed a cab ride to a local hotel (paid for by Arthur), and ordered tickets online to the Louvre (you guessed

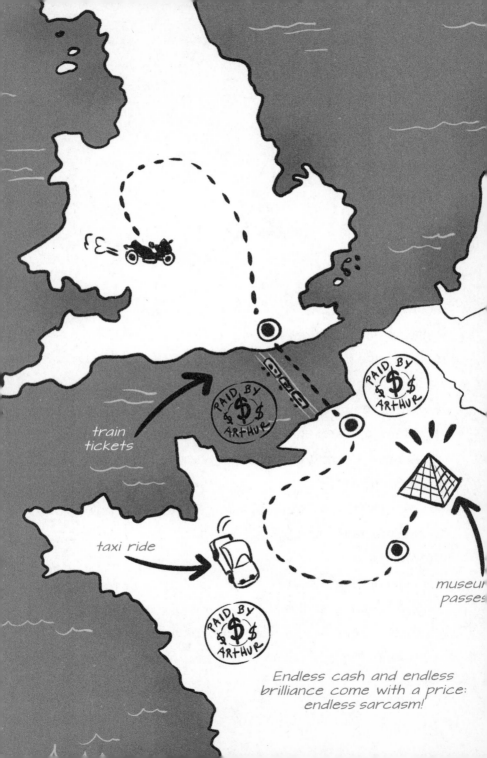

train tickets

taxi ride

museum passes

Endless cash and endless brilliance come with a price: endless sarcasm!

it—also paid for by Arthur). From there, we'd walked right through the front door of the museum with the other tourists and even had croissants and hot chocolate at the ridiculously expensive café on the premises.

Did you know that being on the run from British intelligence was so expensive?

In case you haven't guessed it yet, along with providing some exceptional deductions and perfectly timed glitter bombs, Arthur was covering the costs of our operation.

And we couldn't have gotten to this moment without him.

Hiding in a bathroom, once again.

"Are you sure this will work?" Leo squirmed. "Invisibility cloaks are for wizards, not geniuses."

"You take that back!" Bert demanded. "Wizards may seem cool in books, but real magic takes place at an atomic level! You should be thankful I was smart enough to actually grab my backpack when we were chased out of our safe house, while *you* were too concerned with your mac and cheese, bud."

"The only reason you have this thing is because you forgot it was in your backpack, because it's *invisible*," Leo quipped.

Bert rolled his eyes. As the tallest one of us, he had

the hardest time in such a cramped situation. And yes, you read that right—we were officially hiding in the fancy bathroom of the Louvre, waiting for closing time. Bert hunched down and tried to keep his toes buried beneath one of the super high-tech cloaks he'd shown up with.

"I told you! It's *not* an invisibility cloak!" Bert whined. "It's a *spectral cloak*. It changes light waves as they pass through an object!"

"Therefore creating the illusion of . . ." Leo teased.

Bert pouted. "Invisibility. *Fine.*"

With three of us to conceal, Bert's cloaking experiments were getting a real workout. We'd broken up into three groups, with Leo, Bert, and me under one; Charlie, Grace, and Mary under a second one; and Mo and Artie under the third. Each group was in a different bathroom all over the museum. According to Leo's research, museum staff usually checked the bathrooms a few minutes before closing on a specific schedule, and then once more around eleven thirty, after the museum doors were finally locked for the night.

"Grace, can you hear me?" I checked the GeckoDot on my ear again and kept my voice low. Ever since I'd first led Agent Donnelly to our safe house back in London, I couldn't shake the feeling that he was snapping at my heels like a rabid dog, triangulating our positions somehow.

"Loud and clear, Nikki," Grace said. "Is everyone else connected?"

I counted off the voices in my ears as the rest of the team chimed in, one at a time, to confirm they could hear Grace's instructions.

"Is Pickles behaving, Charlie?"

"She's currently sawing logs in my backpack, Nikki," Charlie answered. "I promise. No matter what happens, I'll keep her safe!"

I nodded once to myself. With Mary so wound up in Victoria's past, I'd passed my beloved pet over to Charlie. I wanted to be able to focus on Mary tonight, just in case.

"We've got about two minutes until security does the final check of the bathrooms," Grace said. "Everyone stay put. After that, we'll head to the guard's station, disable the cameras around the Venus de Milo, and get our butts over to the statue as quickly as we can."

Bert sucked in a loud breath, loosening his shirt collar. "And what if Victoria's released the serum into the air already, huh? We could all be breathing it in right now and have no idea!"

My chest constricted at the thought of some horrible virus coursing through my bloodstream without me knowing it, but Mary's voice abruptly cut off that nightmare.

"No way," she said. "After everything we've been through, she clearly wants us to be there when it happens. I'm sure of it."

I nodded to myself. If anything, I was happy to hear Mary getting some of her usual quiet confidence back.

"Everyone!" Grace hissed. "Shh! Not a word until *all* areas have been cleared."

Sure enough, it wasn't long before the patter of thick-soled shoes entered the restroom where we were hiding. There was a slight shift in Bert's cloak on my shoulders as we all inhaled deeply and held our breaths.

The guard hummed over the squeaking doors of each stall as he checked for stragglers.

Suddenly, the jarring sound of electronic jazz filled the room.

What the?! My eyes widened as I looked to Leo for answers.

"Bonjour?" the guard greeted. "Hello?"

My heart shot up to my throat. The sharp intake of my gasp shifted the cloak ever so slightly, causing Bert to squeeze my hand and point to the ground. I ducked down until the cloak covered the tips of his shoes again.

A low, annoyed huff filled the restroom, sending another jolt up my spine.

Whoever he was talking to, the guard was *not* pleased.

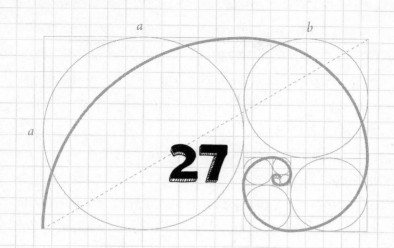

27

Moving as slowly as he dared, Leo bent his arm to set his hand next to his head, mimicking a telephone.

Ohhhh.

My knees buckled under me. The guard was taking a *phone call.*

See, I told you I was paranoid.

From the sound of his voice, he wasn't very old—maybe only in his midtwenties.

"What are you doing calling me here?!" he hissed. He spoke French, but the three of us could translate easily enough. "I told you not to phone when I'm at work!"

Bert's mouth dropped open as we eavesdropped.

The guard paused, and I heard the distinct creak of

one of the chairs situated by the sink. *"Maaamaaan,"* he whined. "Can't we talk about this later?" Another pause. "No, I don't want pasta again," he said. "You promised we could get pizza. Yes, you did! You told me we could get pizza if I cleaned out Sprinkles's litter box, and I did that yesterday!"

"Sprinkles?" Leo mouthed to me, barely holding back his giggle. Then he tapped his watch. I couldn't argue with him—we were going to be late because of this guard—but what could we do? We had no other option but to wait it out and hope that the fate of the world didn't rest upon the actions of a museum guard with a cat named Sprinkles.

fancy bathroom

fancy cloak

not-so-fancy nerds

After what seemed like an *eternity* of arguing about pizza, the cat, and what his brother got for his birthday, the satisfying *beep* of a call ending sounded through the room.

It's a good thing, too, because ten more seconds of that nonsense would have been enough to make me blow our cover so I could throw his phone in the toilet.

The three of us groaned with relief as the restroom door closed.

"That was *awful*!" I whispered, throwing the cloak from my shoulders and stretching my arms above my head. My neck cracked loudly at the movement. "How long were we under there? What year is it?"

"Five minutes," Leo said. He pressed the dot on his collar to check in with the others. "Hello? Anyone there?"

I turned on my own dot and listened. Mary was first to speak. "We're here," she whispered. "And we're headed to the statue now! Is everyone ready?"

Leo grabbed my hand. "We're ready," he said. He was talking to Mary but looked me right in the eye. His tone went from eager to serious. "It's going to be all right," he told me.

For the record? I was *not* okay with our plan. Most of us were going to keep Victoria distracted before she could release the serum, while Leo went off on his own and snuck around behind her. Our hope was that she would count seven kids and forget that we were now a team of eight—giving Leo a chance to make his move and wrestle the serum from her.

"It's not too late," I said, gripping his hands in mine.

"Why don't Charlie and I go with you? We're fast, and three of us will have a better chance than one."

Charlie joined in the conversation through our ears. "Happy to help if you want it, Leo!"

Leo frowned. "I know you're worried, but like I already told you, I'm going to have a much better chance of staying hidden on my own—she'll notice if someone is missing. Plus, we may need every last one of you to keep her talking!" He squeezed his dot once, cutting off the others from listening. "And you've got to be there for Mary," he reminded me. "It's her aunt we're confronting. Her family. She'll need you there, Nikki."

"I want to be there for *everyone*," I said. "You and Mary—the entire team!" I hiccupped, annoyed at the pathetic way my voice cracked.

"Hey," he said. "You *are* there for us. We all know that, including Mary. We've only got one more step to complete this mission. We can do this!"

"Right," I said, forcing a smile onto my face. Despite how torn I was about how best to help my friends, I didn't want Leo to waste any time worrying about my feelings. "We need to finish the mission."

"Just like always." He winked at me.

"Promise me one thing?" I said.

"Anything."

"Whatever happens tonight, make sure Mary's okay," I said. "I'm really worried about her, and I'm afraid Victoria might do something Mary won't recover from."

He squeezed my hand tight. "Of course," he said. "We're all watching out for her."

I steeled my nerves and gave him a kiss on the cheek before watching him dash down the hall to where he'd hide. Midnight was approaching, and no matter how much I willed the clock to slow down, time was running out.

To my surprise, Bert came over and rested his hand on my shoulder. "This is going to work, Nikki," he said quietly.

I bit the inside of my cheek, avoiding his eyes. Nothing would get me crying like Bert being *too* sincere. "And how do you know that?"

We started to slink our way through the shadows toward the statue and the rest of our team.

"Because it's got to," he said simply.

As weird as it sounds, Bert's words actually made me feel better, and my breath began to level out as

we navigated our way to the Sully wing, where the Venus de Milo statue was located.

But my relief didn't last for long.

Instead of the lone Venus de Milo—beautiful yet tragic—bathed in light in the middle of the marble room, there were *two* statuesque figures waiting for us when we arrived.

Victoria had beaten us there.

And worse, she greeted us with a smile.

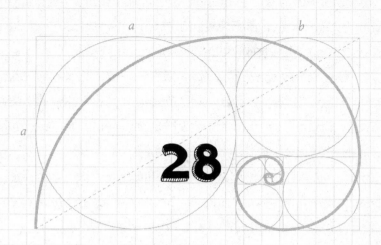

28

She was taller than I expected, with her hair bundled up in a messy bun held together with a pencil. Were it not for the crazed look on her face, I'd say she bore a striking resemblance to Mary. Clever eyes, brown hair, and a distinct air of intelligence in her expression. An odd, shiny silver gun was clutched in her hand.

The rest of the team closed ranks in front of her, each of our three groups arriving with military precision. I sidestepped to be closer to Mary, who already looked sick with worry.

"Aunt Victoria?" she gasped.

"Mary." The word was sickly sweet coming from Victoria's mouth, drawn out like a slow drip of honey from a spoon. "It's been a long time, hasn't it? Since we spent all those late evenings in my laboratory with take-out boxes strewn everywhere. Come." She stretched out her arms. "Give your dear old aunt a hug."

Mary's feet remained planted firmly on the shiny floor.

"Easy, Mary," I whispered, noting her shaking hands. Even though we outnumbered Victoria eight to one, my heart thumped with ominous paranoia. It was clear to me that bringing Mary here—face-to-face with her deranged aunt—was one of the worst ideas we'd ever had. I had to protect her, no matter what it took.

Victoria tilted her head playfully. "What?" she asked. "You're not pleased to see me? I must admit, I was hoping for a warmer welcome from you after all these years."

Grace spoke. "Why don't you—"

"*NO!*" Victoria snapped. Her jaw clenched, and her upper lip twitched to reveal her teeth. "This is between Mary and me."

"Well, sorry, lady." I surprised myself by jumping in. "We're kind of a package deal here. You want to talk to Mary, you can talk with all of us."

"Is that so?" Victoria looked at me innocently through her thick lashes. "You might want to be careful. Mary might seem like a true friend, but she'll turn on you at a moment's notice . . ." The thin line of a smirk appeared on her lips.

A small thread of clarity wound through my thoughts. Mary had been right: Victoria *did* blame Mary for her arrest.

"I was *seven*!" Mary spat. Clearly her anger had started to outweigh her fear. "And I didn't turn on you! How was I supposed to know the neighbors would call the police?!"

"You were supposed to be clever," Victoria answered.

"And *you* were supposed to be home!" Mary shot back.

"I had more important things to see to." Victoria's voice was as cold as the steel of the gun she waved dismissively in the air as she mocked Mary. It didn't look like any gun I'd ever seen—with a wide silver grip and transparent sections along twin barrels. The compartments were filled with a light green substance that reflected the light. Curiously, there were also two triggers, one silver, one gold.

That's when it hit me: It wasn't an ordinary gun at all. It was built to spread the virus. I couldn't quite work out why there were two triggers. One to transmit the airborne virus, and one to inject the serum directly into a human body?

I suppressed the gag in my throat and glanced behind Victoria, searching for Leo.

Come on. Where are you?

"She *is* clever," Bert said. His cheeks were clouded red as he came to Mary's defense. "Maybe you're the one who isn't so smart. Who expects a *kid* to stay calm when her guardian goes missing? Who wouldn't be a little freaked out by your ridiculous attempts to wake the dead? Ever think of that?!"

I cleared my throat loudly. Was he trying to make Victoria even angrier? Grace obviously mirrored my concern, shaking her head ever so slightly.

"Bert," she whispered. "Keep it together."

"*Ridiculous* attempts?!" Victoria flared with rage. "You sound like everyone who's ever doubted my genius! Do you know what I've accomplished? How my research will change the world?!"

Bert snorted. "Sure. It will *kill* people. Big whoop. Way to change the world! It's *easy* to destroy things. People do it all the time! You could have done something truly amazing, but instead you're going to end it."

Victoria's eyelids twitched. "You think I'm destroying the world?" She bared her teeth viciously in a snarl. "I'm setting things right again. They took everything from me!"

Her voice rose sharply, and a flicker of pain flashed in her eyes.

What on earth did *that* mean? I glared at Grace while a dangerous knot of suspicion tightened inside me. The way Victoria was talking made it seem like she wasn't just some out-of-control maniac trying to hurt people at random. It sounded like she wanted . . .

"Revenge?" Mary asked. "Is that what this is all about?! Aunt Victoria, I told you—I'm sorry you lost your work and got sent to jail. You want to hurt billions of people to get back at me, but you can't blame the world for what I did! Can't you see how *crazy* that is? It's worse than setting fire to your own laboratory!"

Something about the disgusted expression on Victoria's face caused a swell of uncertainty inside me. We'd seen villains before, but there was something decidedly different about Victoria that seemed to simmer just beneath the surface. Something shattered and fragile. Desperate . . . but not for power.

Unfortunately, I wasn't clever enough to figure it out.

That's where Arthur came in.

"Mary," he said gently. "She's not upset because she lost her laboratory or her work."

Mary didn't turn to face him. Instead, she stared straight ahead, her eyes still locked on Victoria. The others remained silent, but an eerie stillness gripped us as Arthur's words hung in the air.

"What are you talking about?" I could barely hear Mary's voice above the low hum of the museum's ventilation.

Oh no.

Victoria's grin fractured, and a menacing glint appeared in her eyes. "It doesn't matter now." Her voice was almost robotic, and her knuckles turned white as she clutched the gun tighter.

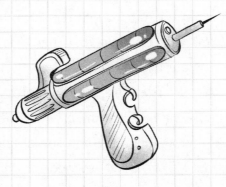

Anger hadn't worked, so now Mary tried something softer. "Whatever you think has happened, we're not here to fight you, Aunt Victoria," Mary pleaded. "Please don't do this. We're *family.*"

For a brief second, a flicker of hesitation passed over Victoria's face, and I thought maybe she was about to reach out to Mary. To grab her hand or give her a hug.

Then the moment passed, and with the Venus de Milo watching peacefully in silence over her shoulder, Victoria straightened her shoulders and glared at Mary with those cold, calculating eyes.

"Family?" she muttered. "You *killed* my family."

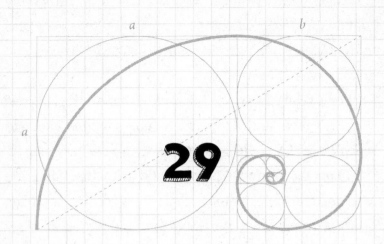

29

"What?!" Mary erupted. Her face blanched. "How can you say that?! I didn't hurt anyone! *You're* the one who designed a virus to wipe out mankind!"

I cursed under my breath, still desperate for any signs of Leo sneaking up behind Victoria. So far, the hallway to the right remained empty. What was taking him so long? Had something—or *someone* stopped him?

Whatever had been holding Victoria's calm demeanor together snapped. "You didn't hurt anyone?!" she shrieked. "He *died* because of you!"

"Mary," Arthur said, his voice rising in urgency. "I tried to tell you."

"What are you talking about?!" Mary's yell echoed through the room, causing a ripple of shock.

"He was the love of my life, and you *killed him!*" Victoria seethed, lifting her gun to aim directly at Mary's face.

"Whoa, now," Bert said, joining me to block Mary. "Let's all just calm down here—how 'bout you put down the gun and you and Mary can actually talk about this, because I'm pretty sure that there's been some sort of miscommunication. Mary wouldn't hurt a soul . . ."

My eyes darted from Mary to Victoria to Grace. Things were unraveling fast, and it would only take a brief slip of Victoria's finger for the worst to happen.

"Oh, there's no miscommunication at all," Victoria said. She sidestepped to get a better view of Mary, staring her down. "Don't you remember, Mary?" Her voice cracked. "The night they took you away?"

Glancing at Charlie—our fastest pair of legs—I discreetly formed a gun with my thumb and forefinger, trying to convey my question. Could we rush Victoria? If we split into groups of three and four, some of us might be able to wrestle the gun away from her while the others restrained her.

But where was Leo?

Without him to lead the charge to distract her, the equation didn't work. We were at a stalemate.

Mary shook her head. "I remember going to the

neighbors when I couldn't find you, Aunt Victoria. But I *never* hurt anyone." A twist of uncertainty had found its way to her mouth.

Victoria's eyes widened, but she appeared to be faraway now, as though the past was replaying on the marble walls behind us. Her chin trembled. "And what then? You told the nosy neighbors you couldn't find me, and the police came and quietly packed up my laboratory? You think that's how it ended?"

"Isn't it?!" Mary threw down her fists.

Victoria laughed. A sharp, serrated thing. "Oh, Mary. If only the world were so kind . . ."

Mary frowned. I could tell by her twitching expression that she was replaying the events of her cloudy past, her memories hidden from the rest of us. "The world wasn't kind to me either! I never wanted to leave. I didn't *want* a new family. I wanted to stay with you! You and . . ." Mary's hand whipped over her mouth.

A bitter smile snaked across Victoria's face. "*Ahh*, now you remember, don't you?"

Mary didn't answer, but her shoulders sank heavily.

"Say his name," Victoria barked. "Don't you dare tell me you've forgotten."

Mary's hands had stopped shaking. "William," she said. "I remember a man named William. He was very kind to me and..." Her eyebrows furrowed as she tried to remember. "And every time I saw him, he gave me a bundle of papers, stapled together in a little notebook."

Victoria nodded slowly. "We were to be married."

"I'm so sorry," Mary said softly. "Truly, I am."

"You weren't sorry the night of the fire," Victoria said.

The world seemed to turn on its axis as the meaning behind Victoria's words settled over me. What Mary had told us about that night—everything she believed—could it all have been a lie?

Mary asked the question I knew we were all thinking. "Aunt Victoria..." she said. "Did you *not* start that fire? I heard the police say that you did it to destroy the evidence of your experiments."

A muscle in Victoria's jaw jumped as she sneered at us. "You think I would set fire to my house... while the love of my life was inside?"

My breath caught in my chest as I pictured the horrible images that Victoria's words conjured. Flames licking the walls, devouring her papers, her curtains, her work... stopping at nothing as they raced toward someone she loved. The thought itself was enough to make my heart clench with terror and sadness.

Suddenly, I didn't feel afraid of Victoria.

I felt *sorry* for her.

"But that means . . ." Mary puzzled it together aloud. "The Franklins?"

Victoria finally appeared satisfied. "*You* brought them to me—to my laboratory—and guess what! Did they wait for the police to arrive? Did they even bother *asking* me about my research?! No! All they knew was what their puny little eyes told them—that a woman was keeping *secrets* and must be stopped!"

"How could anybody do that? Surely that can't be what—" Mary started.

But Victoria cut her off. "They called me a *witch*, Mary! They set my life on fire with the kindling *you* gave them! Whipping the whole street into a frenzy! I returned home to nothing but a pile of singed rubble and the police waiting with handcuffs. William tried to escape, but the smoke was too much for him."

Mary's eyes shone with tears. "Is that why you wanted to reanimate the dead?"

Victoria's lip curled. Now that her story was out, her sadness was getting clouded by rage once more, becoming more lethal by the second. "I had good reason before William's death," she said. "Who hasn't wanted to revive a loved one? I gave up that research long ago. The side effects were too much. But after he died—because of *you*—I had more incentive than ever. I thought the Spark of Life would bring William back to me. However, while it can do many amazing things to the human body, it couldn't do the thing I wanted most. I failed him."

"And when you learned the serum would hurt people?" Mary asked.

Victoria lifted her chin high. "The world doesn't deserve to be saved," she said. "You taught me that. It's only fitting that you be here at the end when I show them all. It started with you. It will end with you, too."

"But, Victoria!" Mary started to step forward, but I grabbed her wrist to stop her. "The whole *world* isn't like that!" she continued. "You can't punish billions of people because you had awful neighbors who didn't understand you. They were afraid of you! Afraid because you're smart! But the best way to show them who you really are is by spending your life making the world *better*, not destroying it. Use your brilliance to help them understand!" Tears streamed down Mary's cheeks as she shouted at Victoria desperately.

"It's too late for that," Victoria said coldly. "They took everything from me. Now I'm going to take everything from them."

Mary was close to hysterical now, and I could hardly stand to see her in such pain. "Please!" she cried. "It was my fault! Kill *me* instead!"

"No!" Bert yelped, grabbing Mary by her other wrist. With Bert hanging on to her, I frantically began searching for a way out of here that kept us all alive. As horrible as Victoria's story had been, I couldn't—I *wouldn't*—lose sight of why we were here. Mourning someone you loved was no excuse for destroying the lives of billions, no matter how much it hurt. It was clear to me now: Victoria wasn't a bad person; she'd just been through the worst life has to offer. Maybe, if we all made it out alive, Victoria could get the help she so clearly needed.

But before any of that could happen, one single pre-vailing fact settled in my mind.

I had to get that gun from her.

Maybe the Venus de Milo agreed. Maybe the spirits and ghosts of hundreds of ancient painters and sculptures of the Louvre wanted to help us that day. Or maybe it was just luck. Because right then, a flash of brown hair caught my eye.

Leo!

He'd finally appeared, sliding closer to us with his back against the wall, ready to lunge for Victoria's weapon.

The others saw him, too, and we all instinctively readied ourselves for what was to come next. When Leo jumped at Victoria, the rest of us could restrain her and take her weapon. It had to work. Failure was not an option.

Sadly, that was exactly when our luck ran out.

Just as Leo got within striking distance—less than ten feet away from Victoria—another figure stepped into view from behind the corner, with a gun in his hands.

A man in a gray suit, with a dark, mottled blossom of a black eye.

"Put the weapon down!" called Agent Donnelly.

Seriously, this guy had the worst timing, didn't he?

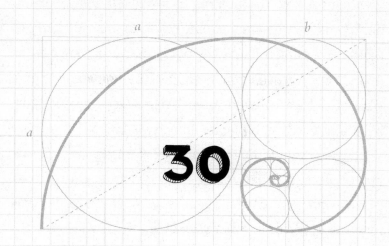

30

"Stop!" I shouted, lunging toward Victoria.

Whatever happened, he could *not* shoot Victoria. Not while she had the serum in her hands. From his perspective, Victoria was a madwoman holding a weapon on a bunch of kids. He had no idea that shooting Victoria would land us all in some very horrible—very *global*—trouble.

"Kid!" Agent Donnelly bellowed. "Get out of the way!" He immediately lowered his gun but kept it wrapped tightly in his hands and aimed at the floor.

"You can't shoot her!" I cried. "See that in her hands? It's a virus, Agent Donnelly. I swear! This is what we've been trying to stop! If you shoot her, she'll release it into the air and everyone in the world will get infected!"

Relief surged through me to *finally* tell him the truth, but it was immediately squashed by the sense of dread that accompanied it. Who would believe us now? After everything Agent Donnelly thought he knew about me? About us? I wasn't even sure if *I'd* believe some kid ranting about viruses and global infections.

If there's anything that villains have taught me in this line of work, it's that you can always count on them to make your job harder. Naturally, Victoria took that moment to throw another wrench in my plan.

After all, Victoria had plans of her own.

"Don't listen to her, Officer!" she said coldly. "My name is Victoria Wollstonecraft. This has nothing to do with you."

"The virus is real," Mary joined in. "You can't shoot her! She doesn't know what she's doing! She's *in pain!*" Mary waved her hands, drawing Agent Donnelly's attention. "Please! She's my aunt!"

"Enough!" Agent Donnelly said, exasperated. He looked to Victoria, demanding her attention directly. "Ma'am, put the weapon *down*, and nobody will get hurt."

This was it then, the moment of truth.

How far would Victoria go to spread her horrible serum? Would seeing Agent Donnelly change her mind?

I could only hope that sharing her story with Mary had been enough.

But all the emotion she'd shown to us earlier had disappeared. She continued to hold the gun in her right hand, completely unfazed by Agent Donnelly's threats. Her gaze turned back to Mary, and a distinct air of sadness appeared in her otherwise vacant eyes.

Please, no.

"This has nothing to do with you," she repeated calmly.

I swallowed down my dread, locking eyes with Leo for a moment. This situation was about to go from bad to worse, and he knew it, too. With Victoria refusing to lower her weapon, Agent Donnelly didn't have a choice.

He tried once more. "Ma'am, put the weapon down."

"Don't shoot her!" Mary yelled.

"This has nothing to do with you," Victoria repeated yet again, that same creepy, robotic tone to her voice.

I didn't need Mary or Arthur's ability to deduce the future to know what was going to happen next.

Agent Donnelly took one final glance at the team—eight kids he was trying to protect from harm—and raised his gun to aim at Victoria. He was going to warn her one final time, and then, when Victoria didn't surrender, he would have to shoot her. Victoria would pull the trigger on her own weapon, and the virus would be everywhere, with us powerless to stop it.

Mary shrieked, bringing all my rabid thoughts down to one.

I couldn't let it happen.

I couldn't let Victoria release the serum. But even more than that, I couldn't let Mary's aunt—her family—get shot. Sadness could do terrible things to a person's soul, and Mary would never forgive herself for losing her aunt. Protecting Mary meant protecting Victoria.

I couldn't hesitate this time.

So I didn't.

Leo's eyes widened as I leaped toward Victoria, ignoring the gun trained on her. I could only hope that Agent Donnelly wouldn't accidentally shoot me.

Crashing into Victoria, I grappled for her weapon, the two of us landing in a heap at everyone's feet, with my team shouting for help and Agent Donnelly bellowing for us to stop.

I grunted in anger at Victoria, clawing at her viselike grip on the gun. Much closer now, I could make out that there were two barrels to the gun, each connected to one of the triggers on the handle. All I had to do was get the

gun away from her before she managed to wrap her finger around a trigger. With the chaos around us, I knew I
had only seconds . . .

I almost had it, too.

But she was too strong.

Grunting in pain, Victoria wrenched the gun away
from my grasp and elbowed me in the sternum, shifting
back onto her feet.

My vision tunneled as the tip of her finger traveled
from the barrel of the gun to the trigger—the silver
one—and the slight pressure of the movement turned
her knuckle white.

"You can't!" I begged, twisting on my knee to kick at
her before it was too late. "Please! For Mary!"

"I can," she said.

And she did.

In moments of grave peril, I've heard that time can slow down. The seconds can become minutes, and every breath gets dragged out until you're left reeling in a strange sort of limbo while the world happens around you.

That didn't happen to me as I lay sprawled out on the shiny floor of the Louvre. Time didn't change.

Instead, it was *space* that shifted. The room became bigger and broader, more spacious than before, and suddenly it felt as though there were no walls at all surrounding us. There were no doors, no windows in the museum. No walls on earth that would stop what was about to happen.

Because when it comes to airborne viruses, there *are* no walls.

Victoria pulled the silver trigger.

A burst of green haze erupted from the tip of the gun, dissipating into the air with a quick fizzle, like the smoke from a match being struck or the sharp burn from a leftover crumb of food on the element of a stove.

Just like that, the virus was in the air.

And in that second, we'd lost.

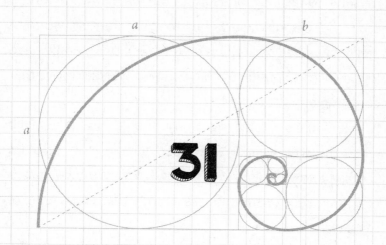

31

In true Agent Donnelly fashion, he had no idea what had happened. All hopes I'd had that he'd believed me were dashed. He was completely oblivious to the lethal virus making its sinister way into our lungs.

"Stand up," he barked. "Both of you! And I swear, if anybody in this room moves another muscle, so help me . . ."

"I'm sorry." It was all I could say.

Was I talking to Mary? To everyone? I didn't even know. The reality of what Victoria had done crashed over me. There was no use going over every detail—every second that had led up to that decision I'd made.

What was done was done.

And yet, I knew I'd never be able to get out of that

museum for as long, or short, as the rest of my life turned out to be. I would always be replaying the last two minutes in my head, searching for the loophole I should have found. The action I could have taken. The one move that could have made it *right*.

I should have felt it, right? You should be able to feel it when the world ends. Your heart should stop, or tears should come to your eyes. But I felt nothing—just a crushing, shocked numbness permeating every one of my cells.

We'd lost. The virus was already drifting through the air, through the ventilation ducts above our head and all over the museum. Within hours, the air would be full of the invisible molecules, ready to infect the millions of tourists who would be lining up at the door at dawn.

And there was nothing I could do to stop it.

"It's over!" Victoria shouted at Agent Donnelly. Now that her virus had been released into the air, she appeared exhausted, her work finally complete. She set the gun by her feet, close enough to place the tip of her foot on it protectively.

"You're infected, and I suggest you go home and make your last arrangements. You'll want to say goodbye to your loved ones, as they'll be infected by the end of the day, too."

"Not you, too," he groaned, running his hand through his messy hair. "Enough with this madness! Now all of you—get your hands in the air!"

The others dutifully lifted their hands, and it was only then—with the shock of seeing them so resigned—that something shoved away the numbness inside me.

What could we do if Agent Donnelly didn't believe us? It was too late for us already. We'd all been exposed. We'd all been infected, breathing in the virus along with him.

But something stopped me from lifting my hands in surrender. Something small and quiet—a whisper of an idea growing inside me, taking control of my body.

The virus was already running rampant in the air. Dissipated into millions of molecules. We'd traveled thousands of miles to chase it down, but it had been for nothing. My head spun, racing through every bit of knowledge I'd ever encountered about viruses. About bloodstreams.

About death.

What we needed—what Victoria had completely overlooked—was an antidote.

We couldn't make one with the virus already dispersing into the air. But that didn't mean this was over.

We needed a concentrated dose of the virus itself. We needed it safe, locked away, and protected so doctors could use it to develop the cure. Right now, that dose was still in the other barrel of Victoria's gun. But what if she realized it and pulled the trigger once more?

The virus would be lost, and all hopes of an antidote gone with it.

I knew what I had to do.

And if you've read any of these official records before, you know that I'm no stranger to doing some truly stupid stuff. I've gotten into all *kinds* of trouble before. I've nearly died dozens of times in my life. But this time? It felt different.

Maybe it's because all those other times, mortal peril was only a side effect of whatever I was doing rather than the end goal. This was the first time that I was actively running *toward* my own demise. That made it infinitely scarier.

I couldn't give myself time to think about it. We were already all infected. We were already all *toast*. But there was still something I could do. A microscopic chance to save my friends.

Shifting on my feet, I found some traction with the tip of my sneaker on the shiny floor. The gun still lay by Victoria's foot.

I debated catching Leo's attention. I needed a diversion—someone to cause enough of a stir that I could grab the gun one last time. But a quick look at his drawn face told me that I wouldn't find any help there—what I was hoping to do was too much to ask of him.

He could never help me do such a horrible thing.

Nobody on the team could.

I needed someone who understood—who saw that despite my plan being ridiculously dangerous, it was the only logical solution.

I caught Arthur's eye and pitched my chin forward slightly in the direction of Victoria's gun.

He blinked in question. *What are you going to do?*

Calmly reaching my right hand to my left forearm, I gave it the slightest tap, like I was brushing away a mosquito. Arthur's eyes widened in understanding and looked to Leo, then to Mary.

He was reading my mind, exactly as Mary would. Saying that Leo and Mary would both act as soon as they realized what I intended to do. For the next thirty seconds, they weren't my friends or allies. They were my biggest obstacles.

To be their friend, I had to become their enemy, just this once.

Arthur began to lean to his right, closer to Leo. He was going to have to be quick if he had any chance of stopping him. That left me to deal with Mary. I could only hope that her fears and confusion about Victoria were enough to distract her.

Mouthing the numbers to Arthur, I started at three. *Two . . . one!*

Skidding my way back to Victoria, I caught her by surprise this time and swiped the gun from beneath her feet in one quick movement. Agent Donnelly, who had not been expecting me to take another run at the weapon, lifted his gun to aim again at Victoria to protect me. Grace, Charlie, and Mo lunged for Victoria in a desperate attempt to shield her for Mary's sake while Arthur lowered his shoulder to stop Leo from barreling into me.

That left Mary and Bert.

I gripped the gun in my right hand. Does your life really flash before your eyes when you're about to die? I couldn't be sure. I saw waves and mountains, laboratories, and the faces of my parents. Then each of my friends, smiling at me.

They were worth it.

Lifting the gun to place the barrel against my left

forearm, I took one last look at Mary, who was now beside herself with terror.

"Nikki, *NO!*" Her scream rang through the air, and she shoved past the others to reach me. A loud thud echoed through the room as Leo shoved Arthur away from him, and together both he and Mary surged forward, their arms outstretched to stop me—to grab the gun from my hands before I could do anything stupid.

I moved as fast as my feet would take me away from them, but to my surprise, it was Bert who sped forward, joining Arthur in shielding me with his long arms, while Leo, Mary, and the others desperately tried to claw their way past them.

Bert and Arthur—finally united in something—were buying me time.

It was long enough to curl my forefinger over the gold trigger and give the others one final look of apology.

"I have to, Mary," I said. "This is the only way. If this doesn't work, don't blame yourselves."

I gave Bert and Arthur a grateful nod.

Then I squeezed the trigger.

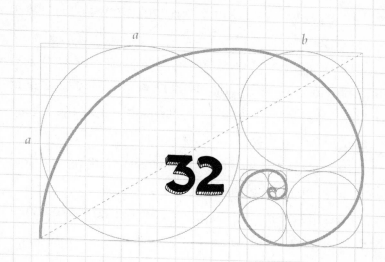

32

What happened next can only be described as absolute madness.

Technically, the virus was already in my body, right? Just like it was already in everyone who was currently in the Louvre. But I was to learn that there was a very big difference between the effects of an airborne virus in your system and one that you inject directly into your bloodstream.

Martha wasn't kidding about superstrength either.

Flexing my hands, I let the gun clatter on the floor. The buzz of blood through my body took on an electric sensation, almost like I could feel every cell. I suddenly saw the small cracks and features in the Louvre ceiling, including trails of dust and long-forgotten spiderwebs in the corners.

I'd thought the Louvre, with its gorgeous hallway and marble floors, was clean, but there were particles of dust in the air floating before me like bubbles in the ocean water.

To my surprise, the serum wasn't making me feel sick; it made me feel *great*.

Pivoting on my heel, I knew I needed to make use of this strength while I had it. I leaped over Mary—yes, you

read that right, *over* Mary—and landed directly in front of Victoria.

"Get back!" she cried. Her boots clicked on the floor as she tried to stumble away from me. "Do you have any idea what you've done, stupid girl?! You'll be first to die!"

I sneered at her, quite enjoying the terrified look on her face. For once, she wasn't in control.

I was.

"If I'm alive long enough for doctors to use my blood and the concentrated serum to develop an antidote, I don't care!"

Well, if she'd been ticked off at me before, you can imagine how mad that made her. My big plan dawning on her, she bared her teeth and lunged at me. If she could kill me, she could stop any hopes of anyone getting an antidote out of my blood.

Too bad for her that she was no match for me now that I had some help from the serum.

Blocking her punch with my left hand, I dodged out of the way and easily grabbed her arms, locking them together in my grip.

"Holy guacamole, Tesla!" Bert exclaimed.

Agent Donnelly watched, stunned, as I lifted Victoria off the ground with one hand and dropped her unceremoniously next to him. "Here," I said. "Whatever happens, this woman is *not* to be harmed. Arrest her, charge her, but do not hurt her. And I'm going to need a doctor *right now.*" I instructed.

Arthur came to my aid. "It's true, Agent Donnelly. You've seen it now with your own eyes. We need you to call the World Health Organization *now.* Get the best doctors in the world, and there's a chance that Nikki really can save everyone who gets exposed. Hurry—with such a concentrated dose, she could have only hours or minutes."

To my everlasting relief, Agent Donnelly didn't argue. He didn't tell us to stop lying, or threaten us with handcuffs. Instead, he pulled out his handcuffs and arrested Victoria, then pulled a phone from his pocket, dialing quickly.

Apparently, seeing a kid leap twelve feet in the air was enough to convince even the most stubborn of agents that *something* was going on.

"Yes," he said into his phone. "This is Donnelly. Get me someone from the World Health Organization."

"I told you that we were on the same side," I muttered to Agent Donnelly, plunking down beside him. The earlier bout of strength I'd felt was slowly waning, probably from the effects of the serum itself and the huge amounts of adrenaline that had coursed through my body in the last ten minutes. Suddenly, I was exhausted.

"So you did," he said wryly, holding his hand over the phone to speak to me. "I suppose a thank-you is in order."

I waved him off. "No need to thank me," I said. "Just release Martha so we can all go home."

He laughed. "You're not getting a thank-you *from* me," he teased. "You should be thanking me for allowing you to carry out your mission without interference." He winked.

"Yeah," I said. "You only tried to shoot me a couple of times and handcuffed me twice."

"Nobody's perfect," he said. "I'll make sure that Martha is released. You'll all be able to go home to Genius Academy. Hey." He paused. "Hang in there, Nikki."

A cold hand touched my forehead, but I couldn't make out who it was.

"Thanks," I mumbled. It was getting harder by the second to speak, and my vision began to flicker. I worked my jaw, trying to find the source of the strange pain in my head. The sound of my heart grew loud in my ears.

Why was the world growing darker? A dizzy, spiraling whir began to twist through my chest, and I registered a gentle tugging on my arm. Someone...holding my hand? The faintest touch of fur tickled my cheek.

"Pickles..." I mumbled. My mouth was cotton. A small ray of happiness warmed me to learn she'd survived the past fifteen minutes stowed away in Charlie's backpack. Charlie would take care of her until I was better.

"No, this can't be happening . . ."

Was that Mary? Her voice was choppy and thin. Like she was speaking from a tin can. I tried to answer her, but air wouldn't find its way to my lungs.

"It's too strong . . ."

"We're losing her!"

"Oh God—this can't be happening!"

The words didn't make sense to my muddled brain. Who were we losing?

One last flicker of clarity rang through me, a bubble rising to the surface of the fog in my mind, long enough for me to glimpse it before it exploded.

Me.

They're losing me.

I wanted to go back to the lovely marble room with Mary and the others. I wanted to pull myself back to them so I could tell them what they meant to me. To thank them for always being there for me, through everything.

My team.

My family.

But the darkness was too strong. The pull of inky black was comforting and terrifying. If I'd been stronger, maybe I would have lasted longer. If I'd been smarter, maybe I would have realized what was going on.

But it was too late, and like usual, the others had figured it out before me.

I was dying.

Two Weeks Later

I don't know who I'm writing this for.

Nikki kept diaries of her life, official government records she said were insurance in case she ever found herself in trouble.

I guess it wasn't the worst idea, since we all have a habit of getting into scrapes from time to time.

I couldn't bear the thought of her mission staying unresolved.

Things haven't been the same with her gone. Genius Academy is up and running again, but our heart is missing. She'd only been part of our family for a year, but none of us know how to go on without her.

I was given her journals last week—for posterity—and while I wish I could relive those adventures with her, even if it's only in writing, I can't bring myself to face them. She was my best friend.

If you're reading this, if you're alive and healthy, it's because of Nikki. She was brave enough to give everything up for her friends and her fellow humans.

Let the record show that Nikki Tesla, however reckless, dangerous, and stubborn she may have been, was single-handedly responsible for saving the world.

Yours,

Mary Shelley

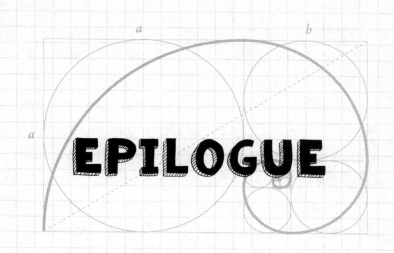

EPILOGUE

One Month Later

Surprise!

I'm baaaaaaaacccckkkk! Things got a little intense there for a minute, didn't they!? I know I owe you all an explanation, but first, let's celebrate the fact that Victoria didn't succeed in ending humanity. I'm alive! You're alive! Hooray!

After I injected myself, Agent Donnelly took over. For some reason, he trusted me, despite the fact that he initially thought I was some good-for-nothing kid at a fancy boarding school. He still maintains that I'm some punk kid, but now he at least accepts that even the government needs to listen to us punk kids *sometimes*.

The bad news? I totally died.

I don't recommend it.

I mean it. My heart stopped. Things were looking capital-*B-A-D* BAD, for several days there. (Did you think Mary was faking it in her note? I told you all along—I would include *everything* in these notes as proof of what happened, didn't I?) Anyway, after I injected the Spark serum into my arm, it looked like I was toast. My heart stopped beating for forty-seven seconds. But thankfully, someone was looking out for me, and emergency services showed up in time to revive me. It took about four days for the world's greatest medical minds to devise a workable antidote using the concentrated virus in my blood, which was then manufactured and sent to every corner of the earth in record time.

It was an "unprecedented" medical event, and Agent Donnelly told me that researchers everywhere were going to want to interview and examine me. Fortunately, when Martha was finally released from MI6 custody, she quickly put a stop to that nonsense. All information about me, the serum, and what happened at the Louvre was deemed "classified," so it didn't even make the nightly news.

As for Mary, she's recovering okay after learning the truth about Victoria's past. Despite the awful things her aunt did, it was hard to stay mad at her. Victoria had lost someone she loved, and that kind of grief is never easy to deal with. Instead of a jail sentence, she was placed in a hospital in a quiet town not too far away from the Academy. She's getting professional help to deal with her grief, and she and Mary have even been writing to each other. It makes me happy to think that, over time, the two of them might be family again.

And Arthur? Well, it looks like we'll be able to visit that castle of his again, as he's officially the newest member of Genius Academy! And get this: It wasn't Mary who convinced him. It was *Bert*. Don't get me wrong, he still thinks Arthur is a total pain in the butt, but even he couldn't deny our team could use those powers of deduction when the fate of the world is at stake. Which brings us to today, in a small garden in Paris, with the smell of spring flowers in the air and a winding aisle of green grass ahead of me.

I once heard a phrase: The more things change, the more they stay the same. I think that must be true, because even though my shoulder still hurts from the injection that saved my life *and* the lives of everyone exposed to the Spark serum last month, I once again found myself in shoes that pinched my toes, staring at my watch, waiting for the music to start.

I adjusted the orchid above my ear, hoping it wasn't

lopsided. Pickles nuzzled against my neck, ready for her big moment. She felt heavier than usual—probably because Charlie had spoiled her rotten with treats during the few weeks I was in the hospital.

"Do I look okay?" I lifted my hands in question and mouthed to my friends.

They each gave me a thumbs-up from where they were sitting a few yards away, waiting for the ceremony to begin. Mary, Arthur, Grace, Charlie, Mo, Bert, and Leo— each dressed to impress for my parents' wedding. Did you think I'd miss it? Well, you weren't alone there. The minute Martha contacted them, they'd flown all the way to Paris to meet me in the hospital. They'd both given me the tightest hug in history and told me they loved me more than anything else in the universe.

But two milliseconds after the hug? They totally grounded me. Even with Martha there to explain the whole thing! Fortunately, I know some geniuses at the Academy who can help me sneak out if I need to.

What would I do without them?

I won't lie. Having that amazing superstrength, even for such a short time, was pretty incredible. The feeling of being able to leap over buildings, chase bad guys, and save the world without even breaking a sweat? I'll miss it.

But if there's one thing I've learned in this bizarre

world of Genius Academy, it's that brute strength is the least we have to offer.

We have to outwit the enemy, you know? The only things that matter are working together to surprise them, using our brains and guts to stay one step ahead of them, and doing the things nobody else can do—even if it means risking our lives.

That's what friends do for one another. They show up and put their minds together for the greater good, no matter how impossible the odds are. And the world is better for it.

Especially because it's got a few geniuses on its side, right?

AUTHOR'S NOTE

All the characters and events in this book are fictional, yet they are based on some real-life people who have had incredible adventures in human history. You may already be familiar with Nikola Tesla (for whom Nikki is named!), as well as the other students at Genius Academy and their real-life historical counterparts. In this adventure, we learn more about both Mary Shelley and Arthur Conan Doyle, both of whom were incredibly talented authors and visionaries.

My reimagined Mary Shelley is kind, empathetic, and infinitely clever, particularly at reading human nature. The real Mary Shelley was equally brilliant. When she was twenty-one years old, she published a book called *Frankenstein*—a name that likely sounds familiar to you, even more than two hundred years later! Shelley's *Frankenstein* was the first novel of its kind, and she is now rightfully known as the "mother of science fiction." Were it not for Mary Shelley, all your favorite science-fiction stories might not exist today! She said she was inspired to create *Frankenstein* after having a morbid dream about a young doctor who wanted to create life by animating the dead. Clever readers might notice that the names Victoria, Robert Walton, and William are all reminiscent of characters found in *Frankenstein* or in Mary Shelley's personal life.

This story also introduces us to a new genius by the name of Arthur Conan Doyle. If you're familiar with the character of Sherlock Holmes, you have Doyle to thank for it. Doyle was born in 1859 in Edinburgh, Scotland. His mother was an excellent storyteller and would spend hours telling tales that sparked Doyle's imagination. Doyle went on to study medicine at the University of Edinburgh, where he soon met a professor named Joseph Bell. He was enchanted by Bell's keen deductive and observational powers, then created Sherlock Holmes from his inspiration. Doyle published sixty stories about the famed detective.

In real life, Mary Shelley and Arthur Conan Doyle weren't alive at the same time (Shelley passed away nine years before Doyle was born), but I have a feeling that if history had provided the opportunity, the two of them would have loved each other's company. Equally matched in brilliance, imagination, and observational prowess, I believe both Mary Shelley and Arthur Conan Doyle would have been capable of impossible things together— including saving the world!

To learn more about the geniuses in this book, visit your local library or bookstore.

ACKNOWLEDGMENTS

Shout-out to everyone who loves books so much, they even read the acknowledgments! As always, it's so important to point out that despite it being my name on the cover, this book wouldn't exist without the help, insights, and guidance of many fabulous people.

To the first-class team at Scholastic: You are an absolute joy to work with, and not a day goes by that I'm not grateful to be part of the Scholastic family. Jenne Abramowitz, Shelly Romero, Dick Robinson, Jordana Kulak, Abby McAden, Keirsten Geise, Josh Berlowitz, Erin Berger, Rachel Feld, Elisabeth Ferrari, Lizette Serrano, Julia Eisler, Anne Marie Wong, Anne Shone, Diane Kerner, Nikole Kritikos, Stella Grasso, Jenn Hubbs, Robin Hoffman, and Denise Anderson . . . I could go on forever! There are so many stages to making books happen, so whether you're involved in editorial, design, marketing, publicity, shipping, or social media (or anything in between!), please know that I adore you and am in your debt. You make this job the best in the world.

Lissy Marlin: Nobody illustrates geeky snark and heartfelt tweens like you—thank you for bringing your particular brand of magic to the pages of Nikki's story. You brought her to life in a way I could have only imagined!

To Kathleen Rushall, my brilliant agent, for always asking "Where to next?" on our little adventure through this bookish life together. Your confidence in me is only matched by your impeccable wit, savvy, and heart, and I couldn't do it without you. Thank you for always being a North Star in the sky.

Finally, a heartfelt thanks to my friends, family, and readers. You've read this far, on the very last pages of a book, and that means the world to me. I hope what you find in my books leaves you feeling curious, powerful, and inspired to chase everything you want in life.

Go get 'em.

ABOUT THE AUTHOR

As a zoologist and author, Jess Keating has been sprayed by skunks, bitten by crocodiles, and victim of the dreaded paper cut. Her books blend science, humor, and creativity, and include the acclaimed Elements of Genius series, My Life Is a Zoo trilogy, and award-winning picture books, like *Shark Lady* and *Pink Is for Blobfish*. Jess lives in Ontario, Canada, where she loves hiking, nerdy documentaries, and writing books for curious and adventurous kids. Jess can be found online at jesskeating.com or on Twitter at @Jess_Keating.